'After _____ _____ we go from h____ ____ at all into a living arrangement? And me—a mistress? It's crazy.'

Aristandros slowly unfolded his big powerful frame from his seat and strolled towards her like a sleek dark panther on the prowl. His narrowed gaze blazed golden and welded to her, homing in on the soft pink of her mouth. 'It's not a problem for me. I find you amazingly attractive…'

'And that's all that it takes for you? Lust?' Ella slung between gritted teeth, with a look of distaste.

'Lust is all that we need concern ourselves with, *glikia mou*.' He lifted a hand and let confident fingertips trace the proud curve of her cheekbone. Blue eyes spitting angry flame, she jerked her head away in a violent rejection of his touch. 'Let's keep it simple. I want you in my bed every night.'

Lynne Graham was born in Northern Ireland, and has been a keen Mills & Boon® reader since her teens. She is very happily married, with an understanding husband who has learned to cook since she started to write! Her five children keep her on her toes. She has a very large dog, which knocks everything over, a very small terrier, which barks a lot, and two cats. When time allows, Lynne is a keen gardener.

Recent titles by the same author:

THE RUTHLESS MAGNATE'S VIRGIN MISTRESS
THE SPANISH BILLIONAIRE'S PREGNANT WIFE

THE GREEK TYCOON'S BLACKMAILED MISTRESS

BY
LYNNE GRAHAM

MILLS & BOON®
Pure reading pleasure™

First published in Great Britain 2009
Harlequin Mills & Boon Limited,
Eton House, 18-24 Paradise Road, Richmond, Surrey TW9 1SR

© Lynne Graham 2009

ISBN: 978 0 263 87221 7

Set in Times Roman 10½ on 12¼ pt
01-0709-48081

Printed and bound in Spain
by Litografia Rosés, S.A., Barcelona

THE GREEK TYCOON'S BLACKMAILED MISTRESS

PROLOGUE

'AN ENCHANTING child,' Drakon Xenakis remarked as he stood at a window, watching the little girl playing in the lush gardens of his grandson's villa. 'She reminds me of someone. I can't think who…'

Aristandros veiled his brilliant dark eyes, his lean, darkly handsome face unrevealing. He said nothing, although he had made a genetic connection at first glance. In his opinion it was impossible not to: that blonde hair, so pale that it was somewhere between white and silver, and those hyacinth-blue eyes and pouting pink mouth were like miniature identity-tags. Yes, fate had placed an immensely potent weapon in his hands and he would have no qualms about using it to get what he wanted. Aristandros always kept his conscience well under wraps. Neither failure nor consolation prizes were acceptable to him. Without a doubt he would triumph—and winning most often meant breaking the rules.

'But little girls need mothers,' Drakon continued, his proud carriage impressively upright in spite of his eighty-two years. 'And you specialise in—'

'Beautiful models,' Aristandros slotted in swiftly, conscious that the older man was likely to take a moralistic viewpoint and employ a more judgemental term for the women who entertained his grandson in the bedroom. 'Timon, however, left me his daughter to raise, and I have every intention of meeting that challenge.'

'Timon was a childhood playmate and a cousin, not your brother,' his grandfather countered in a troubled voice. 'Are you willing to give up the strings of gorgeous women and the endless parties for the sake of a child who isn't your own?'

'I have a large, well-trained and reliable staff. I don't think Calliope's impact on my life will be that catastrophic.' Aristandros had never sacrificed anything for anyone, nor could he imagine doing so. But, even if he did not agree with his grandfather's views, he respected him and he would allow the older man to have his say.

In any case, few men had more right to talk frankly on the score of family responsibility than Drakon Xenakis. The family name had long been synonymous with dysfunction and explosive scandals. Drakon blamed himself that all his children had messed up spectacularly as adults with their car-crash marriages, addictions and affairs. Aristandros's father had proved the worst offender of all, and his mother, the heiress daughter of another shipping family, had matched her husband in her appetite for self-indulgence and irresponsibility.

'If you think that, you're underestimating the responsibility you're taking on. A child who has already lost both parents will need a lot of your attention to feel secure. You're a workaholic, just as I was, Aristandros. We're brilliant at making money, but we're not good parents,' Drakon pronounced, his concern patent. 'You need to find a wife willing to be Callie's mother.'

'Marriage really isn't my style,' Aristandros countered coolly.

'The incident you are referring to took place when you were twenty-five years old,' Drakon dared to remark, watching the younger man's bronzed features shutter and chill at that less-than-tactful reminder.

Aristandros shrugged a broad shoulder. 'It was merely a brief infatuation from which I soon recovered.'

Aristandros was, however, pierced by a familiar tide of bitter anger. *Ella*. He only had to think her name to feel that anger. Seven years ago, he had put a price on the head of the one woman he'd wanted, and the one woman he still couldn't forget. He had sworn then that, one day, he would take revenge for what she had done to him. The engagement that never was—an unthinkable rejection. Yet, in some ways, hadn't Ella done him a favour? The early unanticipated disappointment and the sense of humiliation which she'd inflicted had ensured that Ari had never dropped his guard with a woman again. Instead he had concentrated on enjoying the fruits of his fabulous wealth while he'd steadily grown tougher, harder and more ambitious.

His meteoric success had made him a billionaire and the focus of much fear and envy in the business world. Drakon's plain speaking was a rare experience for Aristandros, whose aggressive instincts had brought him astonishing ascendancy and influence over others. Soon Ella too would have to make a bonfire of all her fine, noble principles and prejudices and dance to his chosen tune. He was looking forward to it. Indeed, he could hardly wait for the moment when she realised that he had what she most wanted. That first taste of revenge promised to be sweeter than heavenly ambrosia.

CHAPTER ONE

ELLA sat as still as a statue in the smart waiting area.

Locked deep in her stressful thoughts, she didn't notice the admiring glances she received from the men walking past. In any case, she was accustomed to screening out the unwelcome notice that her physical beauty attracted. Her white-blonde hair, that rare shade most often seen only on children, turned heads as much as her bright blue eyes and slender, shapely figure. Her hands were tightly laced together on her lap, betraying her tension.

'Dr Smithson?' the receptionist said. 'Mr Barnes would like you to go in now.'

Ella got up. Beneath her outward show of calm, a burning sense of injustice was churning in her stomach. Her prayers had gone unanswered and common sense was still being ignored. She could only marvel that her own flesh and blood could have placed her in such a cruel position. When would enough be enough? When would her family decide that she had paid a steep enough price for the decision she had made seven years earlier? She was beginning to think that only her death would settle that outstanding account.

Mr Barnes, the lawyer she had first consulted two weeks earlier—a tall, thin man in his forties reputed to be at the very top of the tree when it came to complex child-custody issues—shook hands with her and invited her to take a seat.

'I've taken advice from the specialists in this area of the law, and I'm afraid I can't give you the answer that you want,' he told her with precision. 'When you donated eggs to your sister to enable her to have a child, you signed a contract in which you relinquished all claim to parental rights over any baby born subsequently—'

'Yes, I accept that, but as my sister and her husband are now dead surely the situation has changed?' Ella broke in with the urgency she was trying hard to keep under control.

'But not necessarily in your favour,' Simon Barnes responded wryly. 'As I mentioned before, the woman who carries the baby to birth is deemed to be its legal mother. So, although you are a biological parent, you cannot claim to be the child's mother. Furthermore, you have had no contact at all with the little girl since she was born, which doesn't help your case.'

'I know.' Ella was pale with strain and a curious feeling of shame, for she still found it hard to handle the fact that her sister, Susie, had pretty much cut her out of her life as soon as her infant daughter had entered the world. Ella had not even been allowed a photo, never mind a visit and a face-to-face encounter. 'But I'm still legally Callie's aunt.'

'Yes, but the fact that you were not named as a guardian in your sister and brother-in-law's wills does harm your case,' the lawyer reminded her tautly. 'Their solicitor will testify that the only party Callie's late parents were prepared to nominate was Aristandros Xenakis. Don't forget that he too has a blood tie with the child—'

'For goodness' sake, Aristandros was only her father's cousin, not an uncle or anything!' Ella proclaimed with helpless heat.

'A cousin and lifelong friend, who putatively accepted responsibility for the child in writing well before the accident that killed your sister and her husband. I need hardly add that you cannot reasonably hope to fight his claim to custody. He is an extremely wealthy and powerful man. The child is also a Greek citizen, as is he.'

'But he's also a single man with an appalling reputation as a hellraiser!' Ella protested fiercely. 'Scarcely an ideal father-figure for a little girl!'

'You are in dangerous territory with that argument, Dr Smithson. You too are single, and any court would question why your own family are not prepared to back you in your claim.'

Ella reddened at the humbling reminder that she stood alone and unsupported. 'I'm afraid that my relatives will not take a single step that might risk offending Aristandros Xenakis. My stepfather and my two half-brothers rely on his connections to do business.'

The lawyer released his breath in a slow hiss of finality. 'My advice is to accept that the law is unlikely to get you any closer to seeing the child, and that any attempt to challenge her current custodial arrangements will destroy any goodwill you might hope to create.'

Tears were burning like drops of fire behind Ella's

unflinching gaze as she fought to retain her self-discipline in the face of that bad news. 'You're telling me that there's *nothing* I can do?'

'I believe that the wisest move in your circumstances would be to make a personal approach to Aristandros Xenakis. Explain the situation and, on that basis, ask him if he will allow you to have contact with the child,' Simon Barnes advised ruefully.

Ella shivered at that piece of advice; it was like a sudden, bitingly cold wind blowing against her bare, shrinking flesh. Aristandros had Callie. Aristandros, who despised Ella. What possible hope did she have of gaining a sympathetic hearing from him?

'Some day you will pay for this,' Aristandros had sworn seven years earlier when she was only twenty-one and in the middle of her medical studies.

'Don't take it that way,' she had begged him painfully. 'Try to understand.'

'No. *You* understand what you have done to me,' Aristandros had urged, diamond-bright dark eyes hard as granite and cold as winter ice. 'I treated you with honour and respect. And in return you have insulted and embarrassed me and my family.'

Gooseflesh pebbling her skin beneath her clothes, Ella left the solicitor's office and headed home to the spacious loft apartment she had purchased jointly with her friend, Lily. The other woman, who was training as a surgeon, was still at work when she got back. Ella and Lily had met at medical school and had been friends ever since, initially pooling and sharing resources, like the apartment and a car, while offering each other support during stressful times.

In common with many young doctors, Ella worked long hours and had little energy left with which to stamp her own personality on her surroundings. She had still not got round to choosing a colour scheme for her bedroom. A pile of books by the bed and a piano in one corner of the airy living-area testified to how she liked to spend her free time.

Before she could lose her nerve, she rang the UK headquarters of Xenakis Shipping to request an appointment with Aristandros. A member of his staff promised to call her back, and she knew she would be checked out since she was not a business client. She wondered if he would even agree to see her. Maybe out of curiosity? Her tummy flipped at the prospect of seeing him again.

She could hardly remember the girl she had been seven years earlier when she'd broken her heart over Aristandros Xenakis. Young, inexperienced and naïve, she had been much more vulnerable than she had appreciated. Her strong sense of self-belief had ensured that she'd stood up for what she believed in, but living with that decision had proved much more difficult than she had expected. Moreover, she had not met another man, as she had dimly assumed she would back then. She had recently begun to believe that she would never meet anyone she wanted to marry.

Was that another reason why she had agreed to donate eggs to her infertile sister? Susie, two years her senior, had suffered a premature menopause in her twenties, and her only hope of motherhood had been through donated eggs. Susie had flown over from Greece to London where Ella had been working as a junior doctor in a busy A&E department to ask for her sibling's help.

Ella had been touched when Susie had approached her with her request. In truth, prior to that meeting, Susie had been as distant and critical of her outcast sister as the rest of the family. It had felt good to be needed, even better to be told that a baby born from her eggs would be much more precious to Susie than a baby born with the help of an anonymous donor. Of course, there had also been the greater likelihood of the child inheriting a closer physical resemblance to Susie through the use of her sibling's eggs.

Ella had not hesitated to agree to her sister's appeal. It would have been unimaginable for her to refuse. Susie had married Ari's cousin, Timon, and they'd had a good marriage. Ella had believed that a child born to the young couple would enjoy a happy, secure life. While Ella had undergone the screening tests and treatment for egg donation, she had also attended counselling and signed an agreement to make no future claim on any child born.

'You're not thinking this through,' Lily had argued at the time. 'This process is not as straightforward as you seem to think it is. What about the emotional repercussions? How will you feel when a child is actually born? You'll be the biological mother but you'll have no rights at all over the child. Will you envy your sister— feel that her child is more yours?'

Ella had refused to accept that there could be anything other than a positive outcome to the gift of her eggs. While she'd been undergoing the donation process, Susie had often talked about what a wonderful aunt Ella would be for her child. But, shockingly, Susie had rejected Ella from the day that Callie was born.

Indeed she had phoned Ella to ask her *not* to visit her in hospital, while also demanding that Ella leave her and her new family alone.

Ella had been horribly hurt, but she had tried to understand that Susie had felt threatened by her sibling's genetic input to her newborn baby. She had written to her sister in an effort to reassure her, but her letters had gone unacknowledged. In despair at the rift that had opened up, she had gone to see Timon when he was in London on business. Timon had admitted ruefully that his wife was eaten up with insecurity over Ella's role in the conception of their daughter. Ella had prayed that the passage of time would soothe Susie's concerns but, seventeen months after Callie's birth, Timon and Susie had died in a horrific car crash. And, as a final footnote, the young couple had been dead almost two weeks before anyone had thought to let Ella know, so that she hadn't even got to attend the funeral.

When Ella had finally found out that her only sister was dead, she'd felt terrifyingly alone—and not for the first time in recent years. Her father had died shortly after she was born, so she had never known him, and Jane, her mother, had married Theo Sardelos six years later. Ella had never got on with her stepfather, who was a Greek businessman. Theo liked women to be seen rather than heard, and he had turned his back on Ella in angry disgust when she'd refused to marry Aristandros Xenakis. The emotionally fragile Jane had never been known to oppose her dictatorial husband, so there had been no point appealing to her for support. Ella's twin half-brothers had sided with their father, and Susie had refused to get involved.

Ella sat down at the piano and lifted the lid. She often took refuge in music when she was at the mercy of her emotions, and had just embarked on playing an *étude* by Liszt when the phone rang. She got up to answer the call and froze in the middle of the room once she realised that she was talking to a member of Aristandros's personal staff. She made no attempt to protest when she was asked to travel to Southampton the following week to meet him on board his new yacht, *Hellenic Lady*; she was simply overwhelmingly relieved that he was actually willing to see her.

Yet Ella could not imagine seeing Aristandros Xenakis again, and when Lily returned from work her friend was quick to tackle her once she realised what she was planning to do.

'What is the point of you upsetting yourself like this?' Lily asked bluntly, her vivacious face unusually serious beneath her curly brown hair

'I would just like to see Callie,' Ella breathed tightly.

'Stop lying to yourself. You want much more than that. You want to be her parent, and what are your chances of Aristandros Xenakis agreeing to that?'

A stony expression stamped Ella's delicate features. 'Well, why not? How is he planning to continue partying with a baby of eighteen months?'

'He'll just pay people to look after her. He's as rich as that fabled king who touched things and turned them to solid gold,' Lily reminded her doggedly. 'And the first thing he's likely to ask you is what has *his* business to do with you?'

Ella paled; a streak of determined optimism had persuaded her to overlook certain realities, like Ari's hardline attitudes and probable hostility towards her. 'Someone needs to look out for Callie's interests.'

'Who had more right than her parents? But you're questioning their decision that the child should go to him. Sorry, I'm playing devil's advocate here,' Lily explained ruefully.

'Susie was hopelessly impressed by the Xenakis wealth,' Ella confided. 'But money shouldn't be the only bottom line when it comes to bringing up a child.'

'It's the size of a cruise ship!' Ella's taxi driver exclaimed while he leant out at his vehicle's window to scan the immense, sleek length and the towering decks of the white mega-yacht *Hellenic Lady*.

'Absolutely huge,' Ella agreed breathlessly, paying him and climbing out on to the quay. She smoothed damp palms down over the trousers of the elegant brown trouser-suit which she usually wore for interviews.

A young man in a smart suit advanced on her. 'Dr Smithson?' he queried, a good deal of curiosity in his measuring gaze. 'I'm Philip. I work for Mr Xenakis. Please, come this way.'

Philip was as informative as a travel rep escorting tourists. *Hellenic Lady*, he told her, was brand-new, built in Germany to Aristandros's exact specifications and about to make her maiden voyage to the Caribbean. As they boarded, various members of the crew greeted them. Philip ushered her into a lift while telling her about the on-board submarine and helicopters. Ella remained defiantly unimpressed until the doors slid back on the upstairs lounge, and her jaw almost dropped at the space, the opulence and the breathtaking panoramic views through the windows.

'Mr Xenakis will be with you in a few minutes,' Philip informed her, ushering her out onto a shaded upper deck furnished with beautifully upholstered seats.

At that announcement, Ella's rigid tension eased a little and she took a seat. A steward offered her refreshment and she asked for a cup of tea, because she thought that if she had something to occupy her hands she would be less likely to fidget. Her mind was rebellious, throwing up sudden memories of the most unwelcome kind. Just then, the last thing she wanted to recall was falling head over heels in love with Aristandros when she'd first met him. She had spent Christmas in Greece with her mother and stepfather, and in the space of one frantic month had lost her heart.

But was that so surprising? she asked herself now, striving to divest that event of any dangerous mystique. After all, Aristandros had it all: spectacular good looks, keen intelligence and all the trappings of wealth. And, in a nutshell, Ella had long been a swot, hunched over her books, while other girls had enjoyed a social life and experienced the highs and lows of consorting with the opposite sex. For the space of a month Ella had thrown her good sense out at the window and had just lived for the sound of Ari's voice, and every heart-stopping glimpse of him. Nothing else had mattered: not the warnings her family had given her about his ghastly reputation for loving and leaving women, nor even her studies or the career for which she had slaved and existed up until that point. And then, at the worst possible moment, her brain had finally kicked into gear again, and she had seen how crazy it was to envisage a fantasy future with a guy who expected her world to revolve entirely around him.

As her tea was served, she glanced up and saw Aristandros poised twenty feet away. Her throat closed over, her tummy executing a somersault. Her tea cup rattled its betrayal on the saucer as her hand shook. She couldn't swallow; she couldn't breathe. In a black designer-suit that was faultlessly tailored to his lean, powerful physique, ebony hair ruffling in the breeze and dark eyes glinting gold in the sun, Aristandros was an arrestingly handsome man. As he strode across the deck towards her—the epitome of lithe, masculine grace teamed with the high-voltage buzz of raw sexual energy—she was immediately conscious of a rather more shameful reaction. Heat pulsed low in her pelvis, and her face warmed.

'Ella…' Aristandros murmured as she got up to greet him, his attention welded to the delicate perfection of her features—the bluest of blue eyes, and the ripe, pink invitation of her mouth. Even wearing only a hint of make-up, and with her spectacular pale hair sternly clipped back, she looked utterly stunning, she was a naturally beautiful woman who walked past mirrors and reflections without a single glance. Her lack of vanity was the very first thing he had noticed about her and admired.

He caught her slim hand in his, long, brown fingers resting against the soft skin of her narrow wrist. Her hand felt hot, his felt cool. That sudden physical contact took Ella by surprise and she glanced up at him, bemused blue eyes connecting with the penetrating dark challenge of his. Suddenly her heart was beating very, very fast and interfering with her desire to show him a confident, composed exterior. She was close enough to catch the faint, musky scent of his skin overlaid with a spicy tang of cologne. That aroma was familiar enough to send a powerful and primitive message to her nerve endings and leave her senses spinning. Her breasts stirred inside her bra, her nipples lengthening as a dart of rampant responsiveness spread tingling needles of sensual awareness through her taut frame. Shame and dismay at her weakness clawed at her.

'I appreciate your agreeing to see me,' Ella told him hurriedly.

'Humility doesn't become you, Ella,' Aristandros drawled.

'I was only trying to be polite!' Ella snapped back at him before she could think better of it.

'You're very tense,' Aristandros husked, sibilant in tone as silk sliding on silk. His attention roamed from her normally glorious full mouth—currently compressed by the extent of her stress level—down to the full, sweet curve of her firm breasts screened by innocuous white cotton. He would dress her in the finest satin and lace; his groin tightened at the imagery roused by that thought.

Clashing with the perceptive glint in his brilliant dark-golden eyes, something trembled inside Ella. In a desperate attempt to distract him, she reclaimed her hand and said brightly, 'I like your yacht.'

Aristandros flung her a sardonic smile. 'No, you don't. You believe it's yet another example of my habits of conspicuous consumption, and you think I should have spent the money having wells dug somewhere in Africa.'

Colour washed as high as the roots of Ella's hair. 'I was a terrible prig at twenty-one, wasn't I? These days I'm not quite so narrow-minded.'

'The Xenakis Trust, which I set up, contributes a great deal to the most deserving charities,' Aristandros confirmed. 'You should find me worthy of approval now.'

Ella paled, because the meeting was not progressing in the way she had hoped. Every word he spoke seemed to allude in some way to the past she was keen to leave buried. 'We're neither of us the same people we were then.'

Aristandros inclined his arrogant dark head, neither agreeing nor disagreeing, and invited her to sit down again. Coffee was served for his benefit. 'I was surprised that you weren't at your sister's funeral,' he admitted.

Ella set down her tea with a sharp little snap. 'I'm afraid I didn't know about the accident until some time after it took place.'

His ebony brows pleated in surprise. 'Nobody in your family contacted you?'

'Not in the immediate family, no. It was my aunt, my mother's sister, who told me after the event. It was quite awkward, because she had assumed I already knew,' Ella explained reluctantly. 'Obviously the news came as a huge shock to me. Timon and Susie were so young. It's a devastating loss for their daughter.'

His lean, strong face was grave. 'And you're concerned about Calliope?'

'I'm sure that everyone in both families is equally concerned about her,' Ella countered.

Aristandros surveyed her with hard, dark eyes and bit out an appreciative laugh. 'Did dealing with patients finally teach you the art of tact?' he mocked. 'I doubt that anyone is quite as concerned as you appear to be—'

'There's something I need to explain about Callie…'

'You think I don't know that you're her biological mother?' The tall, powerful Greek's dark, deep drawl was laced with honeyed derision. '*Of course* I know that.'

Jolted by his assurance, Ella tilted her chin. 'I assume Timon told you?'

'Yes. Naturally, I was surprised. After all, you once told me that you didn't want children.'

'At twenty-one years old I didn't, and when my sole input to the process was donated eggs I didn't consider Callie to be *my* child when she was born. She was Susie and Timon's daughter.'

'How very selfless of you,' Aristandros murmured flatly. 'Yet in spite of that statement you are here.'

'Yes,' Ella acknowledged. 'I would very much like to see my niece.'

'Is that really what you came all this way to ask of me? One single visit with her, and then you walk away again never to look back?' Aristandros outlined with a look of disbelief.

Ella didn't know quite how to answer that. She was afraid to be too honest and reveal the depth of her longing to become a more important part of Callie's life. 'If that is all you're prepared to allow me. Something is better than nothing.'

Brilliant dark eyes rested on her. 'You want so little?'

Colour warmed her cheeks for dissemblance was not her style. She was entrapped by the power of his gaze, awesomely aware of the unyielding strength and shrewd intelligence of the man behind it. She did not dare lie to him, and knew that any form of evasion would be held against her. 'I think you know that I would like more.'

'But would more be in Callie's best interests? And

how badly do you want that access to the child?' Aristandros enquired huskily.

Ella snatched in a charged breath. '*Very* badly,' she admitted. 'I don't believe I've ever wanted anything so much.'

Aristandros loosed a sudden, grating laugh that took her aback. 'Yet she could have been *our* child. Instead, you made it possible for my cousin and best friend to become a father, and let your sister give birth to a little girl who was genetically half yours. Did it ever occur to you that I might find that particular arrangement offensive?'

The colour in Ella's cheeks slowly drained away, and her face took on the pinched quality of constraint. 'No, I'm afraid that possibility didn't occur to me, and I can only hope that you don't still feel that way now that you're Callie's guardian.'

'I got over it. I'm not the sentimental type, and I would *never* hold a child's parentage against her,' Aristandros fielded with a harsh edge of emphasis on that point. 'What I need to know now is how far are you prepared to go to get what you want? How much will you sacrifice?'

'Are you saying that it might be possible for me to establish an ongoing relationship with my niece?' Ella pressed, wondering why he was talking about sacrifices.

A slow, steady smile curved his handsome, chiselled mouth. 'If you please me, the sky's the limit, *glikia mou.*'

CHAPTER TWO

ELLA was thoroughly chilled by the smile on Aristandros's lean, darkly handsome face and his casual term of endearment jarred on her. She had not forgotten what she was dealing with: a very rich and powerful male whose ego she had once dented. Quite accidentally dented, though, she affixed ruefully to that recollection. Their dialogue, however, had taken a sudden step into unknown territory and she genuinely didn't know what he was getting at.

'I'm not sure that I appreciate your meaning,' Ella said carefully, her hyacinth-blue eyes level and enquiring.

'You're far from being stupid,' Aristandros countered in his measured accented drawl. 'If you want to see Callie, you can only do so on *my* terms.'

Ella slid out of her comfortable seat and walked with quick harried steps over to the rails farthest away, eager for the breeze coming in off the sea to cool her anxious face. 'I know that—if I didn't accept that, I wouldn't be here.'

'My terms are tough,' Aristandros spelt out bluntly. 'You want Callie. I want you, and Callie needs a female carer. If we put those needs together we can come to an arrangement that suits all three of us.'

I want you. That was almost the only phrase she initially picked out of that speech. She was shocked. He still found her attractive—seven years on? Even in her sensible brown trouser-suit, when she was stressed out of her mind? In that first instant of astonishment, she almost turned round to tell him that he was the answer to an overworked doctor's prayers. That side of her life had not just taken a back seat while she'd studied and worked her steady path through all the medical hoops she had had to traverse to qualify, it had vanished.

She reminded herself that being wanted by Aristandros did not, by any stretch of the imagination, make her one of a select group. As a woman, she was clued up enough to go on a TV quiz show and answer virtually any question about Aristandros's highly volatile and energetic love-life. She knew that while his sexual skill and stamina in bed might be legendary according to the tabloid press, his staying power outside the bedroom was of exceptionally short duration. Since they had last met, a constant procession of gorgeous supermodels, starlets and socialites had briefly shared his fast-lane, champagne lifestyle before being ditched and replaced. He got bored *very* easily.

Indeed, Aristandros had gone on to fulfil every worst expectation that Ella had had of him seven years earlier. His relationships appeared to be short-lived, shallow, self-serving, and not infrequently featured infidelity. He had closely followed in the footsteps of his notorious father as a womaniser. Nothing Ella read about Aristandros had ever given her cause to regret refusing to marry him. He could no more have adapted to the restrictions of matrimony than a tiger could adjust to being a domestic pet. He would have broken her heart and destroyed her, just as her faithless stepfather had destroyed her mother with his extra-marital diversions. After twenty-odd years of marriage, Jane Sardelos had neither backbone nor self-esteem left.

'You're suggesting that, if I have sex with you, you'll let me see Callie?' Ella queried in a polite tone of incredulity.

'I'm not quite that crude, *glikia mou*,' Aristandros fielded. 'Nor so easily satisfied. I'm even prepared to offer you something I've never offered a woman before. I want you to move in with me—'

'To *live* with you?' Ella echoed in astonishment, a powerful wave of disbelief winging through her taut length.

'Live and travel with me as my mistress. How else could you look after your niece? Of course, there would be conditions,' Aristandros continued smoothly. 'You couldn't hope to work and still meet my expectations. Living with me and taking care of Callie would be a full-time occupation.'

'You haven't changed one little bit,' Ella framed shakily, even as her heart jumped in anticipation at the idea of having the freedom to take care of her niece. 'You still expect to take priority over everything else.'

Aristandros angled back his arrogant dark head, stubborn eyes hurling an unashamed challenge. 'Why not? I have known many women who would be delighted to make me and my interests their main priority in life. Why would I even consider accepting a lesser commitment from you?'

'But you can't make a child part of a deal like that!' Ella condemned fiercely. 'It would be immoral and horribly unscrupulous!'

'I don't suffer from moral scruples. I'm a practical guy who has no plans to get married to give Callie a mother. So, if you want to be her replacement mother, you have to play this as I want it played.'

He was offering her everything she longed for in return for surrendering everything she had worked so hard to achieve. It was blackmail and it was revenge in one cruelly potent weapon. 'After seven years, how can we go from having no relationship at all into living together? And me a *mistress*?' she questioned unevenly, the unfamiliar word thick and unwieldy on her tongue. 'It's crazy.'

Aristandros slowly unfolded his big powerful frame, from his seat and strolled towards her like a sleek panther on the prowl. His narrowed gaze blazed golden and welded to her, homing in on the soft pink of her mouth. 'It's not a problem for me. I find you amazingly attractive.'

'And that's *all* that it takes for you—lust?' Ella slung between gritted teeth with a look of distaste.

'Lust is all that we need concern ourselves with, *glikia mou*.' He lifted a hand and let confident fingertips trace the proud curve of her cheekbone. Blue eyes spitting angry flame, she jerked her head away in a violent rejection of his touch. 'Let's keep it simple. I want you in my bed every night.'

'No *way*!' Ella launched back at him furiously.

'Of course, I can't force you into agreement,' Aristandros conceded, trapping her by the rails with his size and proximity, while staring down at her with burning resolve. 'But I'm a stubborn and tenacious man. I have waited a long time for this day. Many women would be flattered by my continuing interest.'

'Lust is not an interest!' Ella practically spat at him, her scorn unconcealed. 'This is all because I said no to you seven years ago, all because you never got me into bed!'

Towering over her slighter, smaller figure, Aristandros went very still at that charge. His dark eyes gleamed, diamond-bright and hard as granite. 'I let you say no because I was prepared to wait for you. This time around I'm not prepared to wait for anything.'

Butterflies danced in her tummy while rage preoccupied her thoughts and clenched her hands into fists. 'I can't believe you have the nerve to try this on me!'

He closed his hands over her fists to hold her entrapped. He bent his proud, dark head, his breath skimming her temples as he murmured thickly, 'But I always have the nerve in a fight, *koukla mou*. Fighting for what I want comes naturally to me and, if the stakes are high enough, I will risk *everything* to win. I wouldn't be a true Xenakis if I didn't occasionally sail too close to the sun.'

He was so close she couldn't breath, and she was trembling while her heart pounded as if she was running a marathon. He lowered his head to claim her lips and he kissed her slowly with an irresistible passion. Extraordinary, achingly familiar, that kiss was everything she had steeled herself to forget. For a timeless moment she was lost in the heat and pressure of his hungry urgency, shivering violently at the deeply erotic thrust and flick of his tongue into the tender interior of her mouth. Suddenly her body was flaring wildly out of her control, her nipples pinching into stiff, painful buds, moisture surging between her thighs. Memory took her back and she froze, shutting out and denying those shameful sensations while she shifted away from him in an abrupt, defensive movement that caught him by surprise.

'No,' she told him flatly, throwing her head back, little strands of silvery-pale hair breaking free of the clip to brush her cheekbones.

A wolfish smile slashed Aristandros's lean face. He made no attempt to hide his triumph. '"No" is very close to becoming a blatant invitation on your lips,' he derided softly.

'You can't buy me with Callie. I'm not up for sale, and I can't be tempted,' Ella swore, praying even as she spoke that she had the strength of character to make those statements true.

'Then we will all be losers, and perhaps the child most of all. I doubt if any other woman would be prepared to offer her the honest and genuine affection that you could give her,' Aristandros pronounced. 'Although many women will no doubt try to convince me otherwise.'

That final assurance was like a knife finding a gap in her armour to pierce her skin, penetrate deep and draw blood. The very thought of ambitious gold-diggers auditioning to be Callie's mother-substitute simply to impress her billionaire guardian hurt Ella immeasurably and threatened her composure.

'You're being so cruel,' she muttered tightly. 'I wouldn't have believed that you could be so cruel.'

Unmoved, Aristandros surveyed her with hard eyes. 'It's your choice—'

'There *isn't* a choice!' Ella gasped strickenly

'It's a choice you don't like. But be grateful there is a choice to make,' Aristandros urged harshly. 'I could have said no, you can't see Callie, and slammed the door shut in your face!'

Gooseflesh gave Ella's skin a clammy feel. It felt like the cold breath of reality making its presence felt, for of course what he said was true. In the circumstances, even a choice was a luxury, for he might have turned her request down flat. Furthermore, what happened next was entirely her decision. She glanced up at him from below her lashes. He was on some sort of power kick. With the options and offers that came his way every single day, how could he still be interested in her? Was it just the fact that she was one of the precious few to have turned him down? Wasn't that the real secret of her enduring attraction—her one-time refusal, her apparent unavailability? And wouldn't her pulling power wane fast once she was freely available?

'Just suppose I said yes,' Ella suggested in a driven undertone. 'Your interest in me wouldn't last longer than five minutes. What happens to Callie then? I'm there for about a week and then I vanish again?'

His lean, strong face had clenched hard. 'It won't be like that.'

Ella had to gnaw at the soft underside of her lower lip to prevent herself from screaming back at him in disagreement. It was always like that for him with women, wild, hot affairs that burnt out at supersonic speed. 'What would I know about being a mistress? I'm hardly the decorative type.'

Aristandros rested his attention on her, his golden-brown eyes smouldering below the luxuriant black fringe of his lashes, amusement curling his handsome mouth. 'Is there a type? I'm flexible and very open to new experiences.'

Unamused by this suggestive sally, Ella walked back to her seat and sank down as rigid-backed as if she had a fence post attached to her spine. 'If I did agree,' she said very stiffly, 'What would the ground rules be?'

'Your main objective would primarily be pleasing me,' Aristandros drawled, watching her grit her teeth as if he had said something unspeakably rude. 'Of course, there would be no other men in your life. You would always be available for me.'

'The any-time, any-place, anywhere girl? That's a male fantasy, Aristandros, not an achievable objective for a normal woman in today's world,' Ella countered drily.

'You're clever enough to live that fantasy for me. Focus all that career-orientated zeal on me, and you won't find me ungrateful. Give me what I want, and you will have everything that you want,' he traded in a powerful promise of intent.

'Callie.' She framed the name weakly because it encompassed so much and stirred such deep emotion in her. The child she had never seen but whom she longed to love as a daughter rather than a niece. Aristandros might enjoy almost unlimited power over them both, but Ella was quick to remind herself that she also had the power to make a huge difference in Callie's life. And she badly wanted the chance to be there to love and care for the little girl, who had already lost both mother and father at such a tragically young age.

Her rushing thoughts were so frantic and intense, she was beginning to develop a tension headache across her brow. She pressed the heel of her hand there and snatched in a steadying breath. 'How long have I got to decide?'

Aristandros flashed her a punitive appraisal. 'It's now or never. A today-only deal.'

'But that's outrageous! I mean, you're asking me to give up my career in medicine. Have you any idea what being a doctor means to me?'

'A very good idea. After all, you once chose your career over me,' Aristandros skimmed back, keen eyes dangerous.

'That wasn't the only reason I turned you down. I did that for the both of us—we would have made each other miserable!' Ella flung back at him a little wildly, her emotions finally outrunning her self-discipline. 'And let me warn you of one thing that isn't negotiable under any circumstances—if I agree, I will not tolerate infidelity in any guise.'

Strong emotion animated her features, brightening her eyes and flushing her cheeks with colour. It was a welcome glimpse of the passionate young woman he remembered, who had invested so much emotion in everything that mattered to her, but who had tellingly walked away from him without a backward glance.

'I'm not asking you to marry me this time. I won't be making any promises either,' Aristandros delivered in direct challenge. 'I should also warn you that, regardless of what happens between us, I will not give up custody of Callie. Timon trusted me to raise his daughter, and I hold that sacrosanct.'

A half-dozen fire-starting responses were ready to

tumble off Ella's tongue but she held them back, deeming the momentary pleasure of challenging him to be unwise at that point. She was willing to bet that he knew next to nothing about children or their needs, for he was an only child, raised as a mini-adult by parents who had had no time and even less interest in him. Even so, she could not believe that he would do anything that might harm the child in his charge. For her own peace of mind, she had to believe that if she succeeded in forging close ties with Callie he would recognise the damage that the sudden severance of those bonds would cause and make allowances.

'Ella…' Aristandros growled, impatience etched in every angular line of his lean, bronzed features. 'It's decision time, *glikia mou.*'

Ella pictured the imaginary child in her head and studied Aristandros with determined cool. Regardless of how she might feel about him and his methods, she still thought he was drop-dead gorgeous, and that was a plus, wasn't it? But how would it feel to engage in an unemotional sexual relationship with him, particularly when she was totally inexperienced in that line? She suppressed the critical part of her brain because she saw no point borrowing trouble in advance of the event. She forced herself to concentrate on Callie and shut out all the personal, selfish stuff like the injured pride, the fury and the sense of humiliation threatening her. If she gained the right to take care of Callie, couldn't she learn to cope with the rest?

'Okay.' Ella threw her head back and lifted her chin. 'But you'll have to give me time to work out my notice at work.'

* * *

'Are you finished?' Dr Alister Marlow queried from the doorway of Ella's surgery as she lifted a cardboard box from the desk. The room looked bare.

'Yes. I took the bulk of my stuff yesterday.' As her colleague helpfully extended his arms, Ella relinquished the box and then took the opportunity to perform a last-minute check through the drawers. Finally she straightened. 'Will you ask the cleaning lady to keep her eyes peeled for a small photograph? It was of my father and I was attached to it,' she admitted ruefully ' I broke the photoframe last month and took out the photo, and now it seems to have vanished.'

'We'll keep an eye out for it.' The tall, broadly built blond man promised, concerned blue eyes resting on her. 'You look exhausted.'

'There's been so much to organise.' Ella said nothing about the considerable emotional fallout of having to resign from the job she loved. All her years of hard work had been nullified and all her goals had been wrenched from her. She would miss her work and her colleagues a great deal. She would not play any further part in what happened to her patients, nor would she see the benefits brought by the breast-care clinic she had helped to set up. Already she felt lost without the structure of her busy, demanding routine. It had all happened so fast, as by the time her unused holiday entitlement had been added in she'd had only had a couple of weeks' notice left to work.

'I can't say I approve of what you're doing, because you were too valuable a part of our team,' Alister remarked as they walked towards her car. 'But I do admire your commitment to your niece, and know that our loss will be her gain. Stay in touch, Ella.'

Ella drove home while reminding herself that the spacious loft would soon no longer be her home. Lily was buying Ella's share of the apartment. Ella would have preferred to retain her stake in the property, but had felt it would be unfair to impose that on Lily, who was reluctant to take a chance on a new flatmate. Of course she knew Lily would be quick to offer her a bed if she was in need, but it wouldn't be the same as owning her own place.

Just how long would it be before Aristandros tired of her? Her shadowed blue eyes gleamed with resentment, for she was convinced that their affair would be over within weeks. Her novelty value wouldn't last long. Then where would she be without a job and with no home to return to? The proceeds from her share of the apartment would not be enough to buy another property, and she would have to go back to renting again. But, when Aristandros did throw her out, her main concern would be Callie and whether or not she would be allowed to maintain a relationship with the little girl, Ella acknowledged worriedly. She had told nobody the truth about her impending intimate relationship with the Greek tycoon. She had simply said that she was going to help to take care of her orphaned niece whose life was currently based in Greece.

Lily, however, remained suspicious of that explanation. 'I'm trying so hard to understand all this. Do you really want Callie so much that you're happily giving up everything that matters to you?' She demanded that night over the restaurant meal they had organised for their last evening together. 'If it's just that you're getting broody, you could easily have a child of your own.'

'But I want to be with Callie—'

'*And* the oversexed billionaire?'

Reddening, Ella pushed her plate away. 'Aristandros happens to be Callie's guardian and a non-negotiable part of her life.'

'But you do have a thing for him, don't you?' the brunette said suddenly.

'I don't know where you got that idea,' Ella countered with a laugh that sounded more brittle than amused.

'Oh, maybe it was when I noticed you only bought tacky newspapers and magazines so that you could read about him and his exploits.'

'Why not? I was curious because I met him years ago and Susie was married to his cousin!' Ella protested.

Her friend was still watching her closely. 'That last Christmas you spent in Greece before your family started treating you like a pariah—that was when you met Aristandros Xenakis, wasn't it?'

More defensive than ever, for she preferred to hold on tight to her secrets, Ella shrugged a slim shoulder. 'My stepfather made sure we never missed a chance to rub shoulders with the super-rich Xenakis family. I suspect we first met as kids but I don't remember it. Aristandros is four years older than I am.'

'I just feel there's a history there that you're not telling me about,' Lily confessed. 'At the time, I thought you'd had your heart broken.'

Ella rolled her eyes while trying to suppress the memory of the nights she had cried herself to sleep and the days when only work had got her through the intense sense of loneliness and loss. But she had chosen and accepted those consequences when she'd realised that she couldn't marry the man she had fallen in love with. In any case, he had not made the smallest effort to change her mind on that score, had he? In truth her heart had got broken over a much longer term than most. A chip had been gouged out of her heart with every woman that had followed her in Ari's life. But all that was water under the bridge now, Ella reminded herself thankfully. She had lived to see her worst misgivings about Aristandros vindicated; she had made the right decision and had never doubted the fact.

Tomorrow morning, however, she would be picked up at nine, and she had no idea what happened next for Aristandros had not deigned to inform her. Would they be staying in London for long? Would she meet Callie tomorrow? Lying sleepless in bed that night, watching shadows fall on the bare walls, she recalled that Christmas vacation in Athens midway through her medical studies. Time rolled back and plunged her into the past...

Susie had collected her at the airport. Her sister had been single then, and in a very good mood as she'd chattered about the exclusive club she was taking Ella to that evening.

'I've just finished exams and I'm really tired, Susie,' Ella had confided 'I might just go to bed and give the socialising a miss.'

'You can't do that!' Susie had gasped. 'I wangled a special guest-pass for you, so you can't let me down. Ari Xenakis and his friends will be there.'

Susie, with her determination only to mix with the most fashionable crowd, and her strenuous efforts to ensure that her name appeared regularly in the gossip columns, was the apple of their stepfather's eye. Theo Sardelos expected women to be ornamental and frivolous. Ella's serious nature, her championship of her mother and dislike of pretension were all traits that made him feel uncomfortable.

For the sake of peace that evening, Ella accompanied Susie. The club was noisy and very crowded. Surrounded by Susie and her pals, who had nothing more on their minds but the hottest party or man on offer, Ella was bored. She listened dutifully to tales of how outrageous Ari Xenakis was. He had dumped his last girlfriend by text and her parents had had to pack her off abroad to stop her stalking him. As the stories of his wildness, fabled riches and volatility were traded round the table, Ella registered in amazement that there still wasn't a girl present who wouldn't give her right arm to date him—in spite of his evident obnoxiousness. When he was pointed out to her across the dance floor, she registered another reason why he was so disproportionately popular: he was breathtakingly good-looking with black hair, brooding golden-brown eyes and the fit body of an athlete.

If one of their party hadn't collapsed, Ella was convinced that Aristandros would never have noticed her. Lethia, the teenaged friend of one of Susie's mates, suffered a seizure. Ella was shocked by the way everyone abandoned the girl as she lay twitching and jerking at the side of the dance floor. When Ella went to her assistance, Susie was furious. 'Don't get involved!' she hissed, trying to drag her sibling back to their table. 'We hardly know her!'

Ignoring Susie's frantic instructions that she keep her

distance, Ella placed Lethia in the recovery position and made her as comfortable as possible while the seizure ran its course. The other girls disclaimed any knowledge of Lethia's health. Ella had to turn out the girl's handbag to learn that Lethia appeared to be an epileptic and to be taking prescribed medication.

'Do you need some help with her?' someone asked her in English. Turning her head, she found Aristandros hunkered down by her side, his lean, handsome face surprisingly serious.

'She's an epileptic, and she needs to go to hospital because she's been unconscious more than five minutes,' Ella told him.

Aristandros organised an ambulance, his cool in a crisis welcome in the overexcited atmosphere surrounding them. He also contacted Lethia's family, who confirmed that she was a recently diagnosed epileptic.

'Why wouldn't anyone else help?' Ella sighed while they waited for the ambulance.

'I suspect that most people assumed that her collapse was drug-related and they didn't want to be associated with her,' Aristandros explained.

'Nobody seemed to know that she suffers from epilepsy. I suppose she didn't want people to find out,' Ella guessed, her blue eyes compassionate. 'You spoke to me in English. How did you know I was English?'

Dark eyes glinting with amusement, Aristandros gave her a sardonic smile that made it extraordinarily hard for her to breath. 'I had already asked who you were before Lethia collapsed.'

Ella flushed, self-consciousness assailing her, because she was convinced he could only have noticed her because she didn't fit in. The other girls were like exotic birds in their skimpy designer outfits, while she was wearing a simple black skirt with a turquoise top. 'Why did you come over?'

'I couldn't take my eyes off you,' Aristandros confided. 'Lethia was just an excuse.'

'You dump women by text and then call them stalkers. I'm not interested,' Ella told him drily, switching to Greek, which she spoke fluently.

'There's nothing hotter than a challenge, *glikia mou*,' Aristandros husked, black lashes as long as fly-swats lowering on his dark, golden gaze…

CHAPTER THREE

AT NINE the following morning, Ella slid into a silver limousine and watched her cases being loaded. Her hair anchored in a knot at the nape of her neck, she was dressed with care in a narrow grey skirt and a pinstripe shirt. She was well aware that she didn't look like mistress material, but was proud of that fact. If Aristandros wanted to waste his time trying to turn a level-headed unfashionable woman into a seductive bedroom hottie who dressed to impress, then he'd one of those challenges that he so professed to love on his hands.

Ella closed restive hands round the handbag on her lap. Sex was just sex, and of course she could handle it. Technically she knew a lot about men. Most probably she wasn't the sexiest woman around—after all, she had lived for years as if sex as an activity didn't exist. Celibacy had only bothered her once, and that was while she'd been seeing Aristandros. She could feel her cheeks warming as she recalled that burning kiss on his yacht. He was so slick, so practiced, that he knew all the right moves to make. And she had always hated that sense of being out of control. Aristandros, on the other hand, would love getting her in that condition as it would crown his conviction that he was a hell of a guy both in and out of bed.

When the limo drew up by the kerb, Ella climbed out and surveyed the building before her in surprise. The sleek logo of a city lawyers' office greeted her frowning gaze. She walked into Reception, where she was immediately greeted and shown into a room. Aristandros swung round from the window to study her.

'What am I doing here?' Ella questioned before he could even part his chiselled lips. As always he looked amazing, the broodingly handsome image of bronzed good looks and highly expensive tailoring, a sophisticated business-tycoon to his fingertips. But even at first glance he was a great deal more than that, for he exuded a potent aura of power and self-assurance.

Dark-golden eyes narrowed and rested on her, roving from the full curve of her mouth to the swell of her breasts with a sensual appreciation that was as bold as it was blatantly male. Maddeningly aware of his appraisal, and conscious of the wanton awareness tingling between her thighs, Ella flushed a fierce pink.

'I have had a legal agreement drawn up by my lawyers here,' Aristandros informed her. 'I want you to sign it so that there are no misunderstandings between us in the future.'

As he gave her that explanation, Ella went very still and lost some of her colour. 'Why am I only being told about this now? For goodness' sake, I've already resigned from my job and agreed to sell my apartment!'

'Yes,' Aristandros agreed softly, not an ounce of apology in his reply.

Ella worked his agenda out for herself. 'You planned it that way? Now that I've burned my boats, I'm less likely to argue the terms?'

'What I love about you is your lack of illusion about me, *glikia mou*.' Aristandros drawled with sardonic amusement. 'You expect me to be a devious bastard and I am.'

Ella struggled to master her rocketing fury at the manner in which he had closed off any potential escape-hatches and destroyed any bargaining chips in advance. Aristandros was famed for his astute manipulative skills in business and his ability to spring a surprise on his opponents. No doubt it had been naïve of her not being better prepared for such tactics to be used against her. In fact it had not occurred to her that Aristandros might think it necessary to tie her up in some legal agreement, particularly as their arrangement was of an intimate nature.

'Did you actually discuss our future relationship with your lawyers?' Ella demanded, cringing at the idea, and incredulous that he could have gone to such insensitive lengths in his determination to bind her in legal knots.

'I always try to anticipate problems in advance. And a woman as strong-minded as you is likely to cause trouble if she can,' Aristandros forecast.

'But you discussed the fact that you want me to be your mistress!' Ella launched back at him in raw condemnation.

'It's scarcely going to be a secret when you live with me and are constantly seen by my side,' Aristandros responded in a direct challenge. 'I'm not going to pretend that you're just the nanny.'

Air scissored painfully through her dry throat as she dragged in a charged breath, for the level of his insolent indifference to her feelings infuriated her. 'You really don't give a damn about how all this makes me feel, do you?'

'*Should* I?' Aristandros raised an ebony brow. 'How much of a damn did you give when I had to tell all my friends and family that you were not, after all, about to become my wife?'

That controversial question flamed in the air between them like a physical blow. Ella paled, recalling the awful, squirming embarrassment and guilty discomfiture that she had suffered over the whole wretched mix-up that night seven years ago. 'I was *very* upset about it. But it wasn't my fault that you decided to simply assume that the fact I loved you meant I would give up medicine and marry you!' she replied accusingly. 'There was no malice on my part, either. Although I didn't want to marry you, I really did care about you, and the last thing I wanted to do was hurt you in any way.'

In receipt of that spirited speech of self-defence, his dark eyes turned almost black with derision, and his strong jawline clenched hard. 'You didn't hurt me. I'm not that sensitive, *glikia mou.*'

But his anger and desire for revenge seven years on were giving Ella a very different message. Aristandros had always enjoyed a glossy air of invulnerability over a core of indomitable strength that suggested he was too tough to be easily damaged. Yet it seemed to her now that her rejection had wounded him more than she had ever dreamt possible.

'Whatever,' Ella slashed back. 'It still doesn't excuse you for calling in lawyers to talk about the possible problems of an intimate relationship! Is nothing sacred?'

'Certainly not sex,' Aristandros parried drily. 'You need

to be aware that this is not a cohabitation agreement, and you will not be my partner in that sense, so you won't be able to claim anything from me at some future date.'

'Oh, I'm getting the message now!' Ella flung at him, temper racing up through her like flame reacting uncontrollably to a draught, her pride stung to the quick by his assurances. 'You're protecting your wealth, even though you know very well that I have no designs on your wretched money! My goodness, if money had been that important to me, I'd have married you when I got the chance!'

His dark eyes blazed burning gold with anger at that blunt exclamation. 'Here.' Without further ado, Aristandros scooped a document off the table beside him and extended it to her. 'Read it and sign it.'

Her slim legs feeling a tad wobbly in the support stakes, Ella sank down into the nearest armchair. It was a long and involved contract. As her angry resentment cooled, she digested the terms of the agreement. Soon horror at the extent of his ruthlessness was assailing her as heavily as a lump of concrete settling into her stomach. He had reduced their upcoming relationship to the coldest possible set of hard-hitting demands and embargos.

In return for the privilege of looking after Callie and having all her expenses met by him, Ella was to share his bed whenever he wanted while making every possible effort to meet his expectations of her in everything that she did. She was to live, dress and travel as and where he wished. In addition, she was to accept that what was referred to as his 'private life' was none of her business and that interference in that field would be considered a breach of their agreement. Her teeth ground together and she had to snatch in a breath to restrain another angry outburst

The conditions of what could only be called her proposed 'service' were unbelievably detailed and humiliating. How could any man have dared to discuss such confidential matters with his lawyers? Where had he got the nerve to dictate such unashamedly cruel and disparaging terms?

'This….this is outrageous!' Ella told him grittily. 'Why don't you just put a collar and a lead on me and refer to me as a pet?'

'I want the job description to be accurate before you take on the role,' Aristandros traded levelly. 'I am honest about what I want and expect from you. You won't be able to say that you weren't warned.'

As Ella read on, she grew ever more tense and rattled. He was even laying down advance restrictions on her contact with Callie—she would not have the right to take Callie out without his permission and accompanying security. At all times she was to respect Aristandros's position as her niece's sole legal guardian and take note of his instructions. Any attempt to remove Callie from his custody or to claim any rights over the little girl would result in her access to Callie being denied. Ella shivered at that brutal threat and glanced up at Aristandros, evaluating the intractable expression stamped in his lean dark features. No, he wasn't joking about any of it. He didn't want a mistress, and certainly not a partner of equal status; he wanted a slave on a round-the-clock mission to please him.

'Until this moment,' she muttered shakily. 'I didn't realise how much you hated me.'

'Don't be ridiculous.' Aristandros sent her a quelling glance.

'If I couldn't even *argue* with you, I couldn't breathe!' Ella hurled back in response.

'I expect occasional disagreements,' Aristandros countered with the air of a man making a generous allowance. 'But I will not accept continual hostility which might detract from my comfort.'

Ella was mute with dismay and disbelief at the iron rule he was trying to impose on her. The written agreement was a humiliating nightmare. She felt like her wings were being clipped and she would never fly free again. Aristandros was determined to own her body and soul, and control her every waking moment.

'We have wasted enough time discussing this. *Sign*,' Aristandros ordered flatly.

'Aren't I entitled to legal advice of my own before I sign anything? I haven't even finished reading it yet!'

'Of course you're entitled to seek legal advice, but that will hold matters up for at least another couple of weeks and extend the time you will have to wait to meet Callie,' Aristandros pointed out.

'I'm beginning to understand why you're so rich,' Ellie mumbled sickly. 'You know what buttons to push, how to put on the pressure.'

'Of course…' Aristandros spread shapely brown hands in a fluid movement '…I want you and I'm programmed to fight for you.'

'You fight very dirty,' Ella whispered, bending her head to read on, still shocked by the extent of the control he was determined to exert over her. She skimmed through the financial details of the ridiculously extravagant monthly allowance he was offering her, and the even more generous 'severance package' promised as consolation at the end of their relationship. How could she fight him? All that mattered to her at that moment was the promise of seeing Callie, being able to care for her and ensure that the child received the love and security she needed to blossom. She was not prepared to risk losing that opportunity.

'Will you sign?'

'If I sign right now, when will I see Callie?' Ella pressed.

'Tomorrow.'

Ella breathed in slow and deep and got up to put the document down on the table. 'I'll sign,' she said.

He summoned two lawyers and their signatures were duly witnessed. She couldn't look either man in the eye, for Aristandros had made her feel like a whore who was selling not only her body to him but also her self-will. She found it hard to credit that the same male had once treated her with pronounced respect and courtesy. She was convinced that rejection had made him hate her.

'What now?' she breathed when they were alone again.

'This…' His hands enclosed her firmly to pull her to him. Long fingers curved to her cheekbone, tipping up her mouth, and suddenly he was kissing her and instant explosions of reaction were fizzing through her bloodstream. His masculine urgency was incredibly exciting. A savage rush of sexual hunger engulfed her. With a helpless shiver she pressed herself to the hard muscular wall of his chest, impelled by the straining sensitivity of her breasts and the liquid heat between her thighs to seek closer contact. She wanted, needed, *craved* more than that connection. He closed a hand to her hips, tilting her against him, and a low sound of response broke low in her throat as she felt the force of his erection even through their clothing, and her own body leapt with instant answering need.

Aristandros lifted his handsome dark head and dealt her a smile that was pure-bred predator. 'Frozen on the outside, meltingly hot within, *koukla mou*. How many other guys have there been?'

Ella hated him with so much passion at that instant for daring to voice that insolent question that she could barely vocalize, and her voice emerged with a husky edge. 'A few,' she lied without hesitation, determined to hide the fact that, to date, only he could extract that mad inferno of response from her. 'I'm a passionate woman.'

A tiny muscle pulled tight at the corner of his expressive mouth. His eyes were as ice-cold as a mountain stream. 'Evidently. But from here on in, all that passion is mine. Is that understood?'

Not averse to taking on the guise of a *femme fatale*, Ella looked up at him from beneath the long, silky lashes that gave her blue eyes such definition against her fair skin and pale hair. 'Of course.'

There was a moment's silence while Ella gathered her wits and her courage. 'Will you tell me what Callie's like?' she asked tautly.

Aristandros stilled in apparent surprise at the request. 'She's a baby. What can you say about a baby? She's pretty—' He hesitated, as if recognising that more than that superficial comment was required. 'She's, er, quiet, good; you would hardly know she was there.'

Ella lowered her lashes to conceal her dismay and concern at that description. A toddler of eighteen months should be lively, inquisitive and chattering, almost anything other than quiet and unobtrusive. Evidently her niece was still suffering the effects of losing her parents. 'Do you have a close relationship with her?' she queried, reluctant to say anything that he might translate as criticism of his guardianship of the little girl.

'Of course I do.' Aristandros frowned. 'Now, if that is all, the limo's waiting for you. You have appointments to keep.'

'Where?'

'I'm taking you to a gallery opening tonight. You'll need clothes.'

'I *have* clothes.'

'Not to suit my social life you don't,' he parried, drily enough to rouse colour to her cheeks. 'I'll see you later.'

Clutching her copy of the legal agreement, Ella got back into the car. She was deeply shaken by the encounter, which had imposed a challenging dose of hard reality on her. The chauffeur delivered her to a designer salon. Her arrival had clearly been pre-arranged. She was ushered from the door straight into a changing room, where detailed measurements of her figure were noted down. Within minutes a selection of garments was being brought for her to try on.

'And for the event this evening,' the senior sales-assistant murmured, fanning an elegant black cocktail-frock out in front of Ella like a bait to hook a fish, 'Mr Xenakis particularly liked this one.'

Ella breathed in deep to hold in an instant desire to state that the dress wasn't her style at all. In fact, she was stunned by the awareness that Aristandros had taken so personal an interest in what she was to wear. He had actually torn himself from the world of business to consider her appearance? Was that the true definition of a womanizer—a guy so tuned in to the female body that even choosing clothing could become a prelude to sex? She focused her anxious thoughts on Callie and achieved a state of grace equal to the task of donning the dress without comment. She was equally tolerant of every other piece of apparel presented to her, even the absurd collection of silky, frivolous lingerie. The new wardrobe was only a prop to enable her to play a part, she told herself soothingly. Unfortunately, the prospect of slipping into flimsy provocative underwear for Aristandros's benefit put Ella into a mood close to panic. Suddenly she was wishing she hadn't claimed a level of experience she didn't have.

The chauffeur took her to a beauty salon next. Ella had no objection to a little fine grooming. Indeed, it was a treat to have someone else do her hair and her nails, and the process of being made up by a professional beautician intrigued her. Colours and techniques were employed that she would never have dreamt of trying. Not for nothing had Aristandros called her '*koukla mou*'—my doll—she reasoned wryly. She was no longer required to be herself. Instead she was to be what Aristandros wanted her to be: a painted, pampered ultra-feminine remake of her former self programmed to behave like the mistress equivalent of a Stepford wife.

In an underground car-park, she got out of the limousine and was ushered into a lift. Aristandros lived in a tri-level penthouse apartment that overlooked Hyde Park. Luxurious acres of space seemed to run off in every direction from the imposing entrance-hall. She and her shopping were taken straight to the master bedroom. A swimming pool gleamed beyond the patio doors, alongside a sun terrace and the lush greenery of a rooftop garden. A maid, who addressed her in Greek, proudly demonstrated the lavish appointments of the dressing room where her clothes were to be stored, before showing her the opulent marble bathroom.

Ella discovered that she couldn't take her attention off the massive bed that occupied centre-stage in the bedroom. The divan was so big Aristandros would have to chase her round it to capture her, she thought crazily, her heart starting to beat very, very fast. Sex with Aristandros—something she had dreamt about seven years earlier and now cringed at the threat of, she acknowledged ruefully. Still, if practice made perfect, he ought to be better in bed than most.

The maid hung the black dress in readiness, while Ella selected a turquoise voile-and-lace bra and matching panties and then went for a shower. When she had put on these items, she posed in front of the bathroom mirror, noticing how the clinging fabric of the underwear clung to the fullness of her breasts and the swell of her hips, not to mention even more personal parts. Just then, the door opened without warning. A gasp was snatched from her parted lips, and she snatched up a towel to conceal her only partially clothed body. Her startled blue gaze was very wide.

Aristandros was in the doorway, seeming taller and

more powerfully built than ever. Having already discarded his jacket, his tie and his shoes, he was an aggressively masculine sight with his shirt hanging loose to frame a muscular brown slice of hair-roughened chest. 'You should have locked the door if you didn't want company,' he teased, eyeing the big white towel she was clutching to her chest with feverish hands. 'For a woman who has been with, and I quote *a few* men, you're very shy.'

Pride stiffened Ella's backbone and she flung her head high, blade-straight white-blonde hair feathering in a silken swathe across her flushed cheekbones. 'I don't have a shy bone in my body!'

'Drop the towel and prove it,' he advised lazily.

In a convulsive movement, her slim fingers released their grip and the towel tumbled to the marble floor. She knew it was silly, but she felt ten times more naked and self-conscious in the fancy lingerie than she would have felt in her own unadorned skin.

Aristandros looked, and made no attempt to hide the fact that he was looking and enjoying the view of her scantily clad curves. Her body tingled in all the private places as though a flame had passed too close to her skin. 'It pays to undress you, *glikia mou.*'

Ella dragged in a charged breath, the creamy swell of her breasts stirring, her swollen nipples visible below the lace. His brilliant eyes smouldered gold, and her mouth ran dry as he took a step forward and reached for her, sinking his hands below her hips to lift her up and settle her down on the marble vanity-unit as if she weighed no more than a child's toy.

'What are you doing?' she demanded.

'Appreciating you,' Aristandros husked, breathing in the soapy fresh scent of her skin as he bent over her, the hot blood pooling at his groin. *His* soap from *his* shower, *his* woman, right where she belonged. It was a moment of supreme sensual satisfaction for Ari. He pressed his warm mouth lightly to the tender skin at her collarbone, where a tiny pulse was beating out her tension. With the tip of his tongue he tasted her. His hands slid from her slim shoulders to brush the bra cups down and ease her pert breasts free of confinement. The sweetly curved mounds spilled forward, held high by the constraint of the bra, the stiff, pink crests drawing his attention.

'You're perfect.' He moulded the ripe swell of her brazenly exposed flesh and kneaded the tender tips. Taken by surprise, Ella was defenceless, mentally unprepared for a sexual challenge before nightfall. Her nipples were unbearably sensitive. Her head tipped back, and a moan broke from her throat as he stroked and pinched the distended buds. A warm, rich wave of sensational response was engulfing her even before he lowered his head to suck the rosy crests. Her control was sliding as inexorably as night followed day. Desire was sinking taloned claws of need into her treacherous body. He drove her lips apart with sudden mesmeric urgency, his tongue plundering the moist interior of her mouth while his skilled fingers traced the taut, damp stretch of material between her thighs and made her shiver violently.

At an unhurried pace, he eased below the triangle of fabric and circled the most sensitive point, teasing and toying with her delicate flesh. All lingering remnants of self-discipline were wrenched from her as he subjected her to his erotic mastery. Very soon she reached the stage where she could have wept with frustration and begged him on her knees for satisfaction. A husky sound of amusement broke from him as she dragged him closer with frantic hands, seeking the temporary consolation of physical contact that their position denied her.

'Take a deep breath, *khriso mou*,' Aristandros urged thickly. 'We have a gallery opening to attend, and I need a shower—'

'A gallery opening?' Only with the greatest difficulty did Ella extract herself from the all-encompassing sexual hunger that he had induced and return to reason again. It was like coming out of a coma to a brash new world. She was appalled to appreciate that Aristandros had virtually seduced her in his bathroom and was now trying to head for the shower while she still clung to him. She whipped her hands from him as though she had been burnt. 'Of course.'

'We have no time.' Aristandros lifted her down from the marble unit-top with strong hands. 'I don't want to treat you like a takeaway,' he murmured huskily. 'I want to enjoy you like a feast and appreciate every nuance.'

'A takeaway!' Ella repeated through gritted teeth of disdain.

Aristandros gazed down at her with shimmering golden-brown eyes fringed with spiky black lashes. 'You want me,' he countered with hard satisfaction. 'A time will come when you don't care *how* I take you…only that I do.'

That frightening forecast trickled down her taut spine like ice-water. 'Never,' she swore. 'I'd sooner die!'

A wolfish smile slashed his beautifully shaped mouth. 'I know women; I'm never wrong…'

'You were *once*,' Ella reminded him before she could think better of summoning up a recollection that could only alienate him.

His lean, dark face tensed, ruthless eyes cool on her face. 'Don't go there,' he warned her softly.

A deep chill formed inside her tummy. Regretting her incautious words, she turned her head away, shame and uncertainty clouding her blue eyes as she returned to the bedroom. For a split second she was recalling the short-lived joy of the moment when he had told her that he wanted her to marry him. Her happiness had turned to horror an instant later when he made a public announcement about their plans while spelling out the fact that she would be giving up medicine to concentrate on being a wife and a mother. Minutes later they had been engaged in a heated dispute in which it had swiftly become clear that Aristandros could be as inflexible in his expectations as a solid-granite rock and quite unapologetic about the fact too.

Rejection had swiftly followed her refusal to conform seven years back. Aristandros was very black and white. There was no going back with him, no halfway measures or compromises. The break-up had felt as swift, cruel and unjust as a sudden death. At least this time around, she reflected heavily, she knew what to expect if she crossed the line with Aristandros Xenakis. There would be no second chance to get it right…

CHAPTER FOUR

'I ALMOST forgot,' Aristandros remarked, striding into a book-lined room off the imposing hall and leaving Ella to hover in the doorway.

Ella watched him lift a small shallow case from the desk. Her smooth brow pleated.

'Come here,' he urged with his usual impatience. 'You can't go out without jewels.'

'I don't have any,' she confided with an uneasy laugh.

'I'm starting off your collection, *glikia mou*.' Aristandros detached the glittering diamond necklace from its velvet bed as she approached him on stiff legs. 'Turn round.'

'I don't want it!' Ella told him sharply for, while she had tolerated the clothing, a dazzling river of diamonds felt too much like the biblical wages of sin. Her principles had already taken enough of a hit.

'But it is my wish that you wear it,' Aristandros spelt out, purposeful fingers curving to her shoulder to flip her round. The jewels felt very cold against her skin. She shivered as his fingertips brushed her nape. He spun her back round and, with a satisfaction undiminished by her bleak expression, surveyed the glittering tracery of jewels encircling her throat

Ella was surprised by the crush at the gallery opening. She had never dreamt that she would see so many well-dressed people and famous celebrity faces grouped in the same place. Nor had she ever received quite so much personal attention for, the moment she entered the room by Aristandros's side, every female head seemed to swivel in their direction. An audible buzz of conjecture accompanied their passage through the crowds. While Ari was engaged in discussing a sculpture with its creator, Ella strayed across the room. She was studying an enchanting painting of the seashore when she was accosted by a tall, leggy redhead whose perfect body was adorned by a tiny white satin dress.

'So, *you're* my replacement!' the woman snapped, settling her furious and accusing green gaze on Ella. 'Who the hell are you? Exactly *when* did Aristandros meet you?'

Ella knew exactly who the beautiful redhead was. Her name was Milly, she was a top model and probably Aristandros's most recent ex. Ella said nothing, for she had seen the tears in the other woman's eyes and recognised her distress.

'You won't get any warning that it's over. One day you're *in*, and the world's your oyster, and the next you're *out* and there's nothing you can do about it. He doesn't take your calls any more,' Milly recited chokily. 'Every door slams in your face!'

'There has to be many safer and more rewarding options for a woman as young and beautiful as you are,' Ella told her bracingly. 'Don't give him the satisfaction of knowing that you care.'

Milly studied her in wide-eyed bewilderment. 'You're being nice to me? Aren't you jealous?'

'No,' Ella declared with innate dignity. 'I'm not the jealous sort.'

Too late, she saw that the redhead's attention had shifted from her.

'Milly.' From behind Ella, Aristandros greeted the other woman politely.

'You're *not* jealous?' Aristandros queried in near disbelief as his ex-girlfriend vanished speedily back into the crush, unnerved by his ice-cold appraisal.

'Of course not,' Ella assured him, thinking of the seven years she had spent reading about his exploits with countless other women. Familiarity, she was convinced, had brought tolerance and common sense to her outlook. Everywhere Aristandros went, he was a target for ambitious women. That was a fact of life, and as long as he remained fabulously rich and gorgeous, the situation wasn't likely to change any time soon.

Dark eyes sardonic, Aristandros guided her back to the landscape of the seashore. 'It reminds me of Lykos…the beach below the house,' he remarked, inclining his imperious head to the gallery owner hovering a few feet away. 'We'll take it.'

Aristandros had inherited the Greek island of Lykos from his mother's side of the family. Once Ella had had a picnic there with him, and suddenly the years were rolling back inside her head and she was remembering how the breeze had whipped wildly at her hair while they ate. Wrapped up warm for the winter temperatures, she had listened with interest while Aristandros had outlined his plans to revitalise the island's failing economy and prevent the population from falling any further. His sense of responsibility for the small, isolated community living on Lykos had impressed her a great deal.

'Where will you hang the seascape?' Aristandros asked as they left the gallery.

'Where will *I* hang it?' she stressed in confusion. 'Are you saying that you are buying it for *me*?'

'Why not?'

'Because I don't want you buying stuff like that for me; the way you're splashing out cash on me is indecent!' Ella hissed frantically under her breath as they headed across the pavement to the silver limousine awaiting them. Crash barriers prevented the gathered members of the press from getting too close.

Her spine rigid, Ella blinked like an owl while cameras went off all around them, and questions and comments were hurled at Aristandros. Uppermost were the demands to know the identity of his new companion. But, in every way, Aristandros remained gloriously impervious to the media presence, settling into the limo beside her, 'Of course I'm going to buy you things; get used to it!'

'I'm only here with you because of Callie. Contact with her is the *only* reward I want,' Ella proclaimed, uneasy fingers brushing the diamond necklace in meaningful emphasis of the point.

The smooth planes of his lean features took on a cold, sardonic light, his brilliant gaze narrowing. 'No man wants to be told that his only attraction is an eighteen-month-old baby, *khriso mou*.'

Ella lifted her pale head high. 'Even if it's the truth?'

'But it's not the truth, it's an outright lie for which

you should hang your head in shame,' Aristandros traded without hesitation, his beautifully shaped mouth curling with derision. 'You want me as much now as you wanted me seven years ago. Don't make the child your excuse.'

Ella had lost colour. 'It's not an excuse. I may occasionally find you…attractive, but I wouldn't have done anything about it.'

'Too spineless?' Aristandros sent her a contemptuous glance. 'I didn't meet your narrow-minded requirements, so the fact that you wanted me and I wanted you meant nothing to you.'

'Don't be ridiculous…of course it meant something!' Ella flashed back. 'But you wanted me to be something I couldn't be.'

Aristandros closed a strong hand over hers to force her to turn and look at him. 'I only wanted you to be a *woman*, not a strident feminist—'

Ella sent him a flaming look of bone-deep resentment. 'I was never strident. I was sensible. We wanted totally different things out of life. It could never have worked.'

'No doubt time will tell,' Aristandros fielded very drily, releasing his hold on her hand.

The silence that laced their return to the penthouse gnawed at Ella's nerves. She was already wishing that she didn't speak first and think later. They were about to share the same bed, and she could barely believe that, never mind accept the idea in the mood she was in. 'If the painting's to be mine, I'll be hanging it here somewhere,' she told him abruptly, surrendering to a sudden need to bridge an atmosphere filled with tense, uneasy undertones. 'Because I don't have anywhere else to live at present.'

Aristandros sent her a sudden, satisfied smile, as if that bleak assurance was a heart warming plus on his terms. 'You live where I live now.'

An involuntary shiver ran down her taut spine as the level of dependency that that statement suggested continued to chill Ella and her independent soul to the marrow.

The tall, powerful Greek closed his hands over hers to turn her back to face him. Brilliant golden-brown eyes assailed hers. 'Don't fight the inevitable, *glikia mou*. Embrace these changes in your life. You might even find that you come to enjoy them.'

'*Never*,' Ella swore in a fierce undertone.

'I hear words on your lips that no other woman has ever dared to confront me with,' Aristandros confided, his deep drawl silky with indulgence. 'You are truly unique.'

Recognising his triumph at the position he had her in, Ella shut her eyes tight. So, when his mouth came down on hers without warning, her only weapon was her rage. But even as she braced her hands to his chest to push him angrily away she thought better of that move. She had made a devil's bargain, and now payment was due. While Aristandros kissed her, she stood like a statue, unresponsive as stone. But he played with her mouth, soft one moment, teasing the next, and then hot and male and hungry, until her thoughts were no longer clear and her resistance was breaking down, sensual response beginning to quiver through her treacherous body in an ever-swelling tide.

With a masculine growl of approval, Aristandros bent down and lifted her, swinging her up into his arms with easy strength to carry her into the master bedroom.

Her heart was racing so fast she couldn't catch her

breath. When he set her down, she kicked off her shoes. A soft glide of air brushed her backbone as her dress was unzipped. His sensual mouth was like a brand on hers. The slide of his tongue between her parted lips was an indescribable aphrodisiac that sent darts of heat and tingles of excitement quivering through her entire body. For an instant she was shattered by the awareness that she wanted him as fiercely as she wanted air to breathe. Guilty unease filtered through her, cooling her head for a moment as she tasted the bitter truth that she was weaker than she had thought she would be.

'Stop it,' Aristandros growled, scorching dark-golden eyes raking her troubled face.

'Stop what?'

'Thinking whatever you're thinking which is suddenly giving you all the animation of an Egyptian mummy.'

Discomfited colour bloomed across her cheekbones.

'In fact, don't think at all,' Aristandros urged forcefully. 'This is sex. You don't need to carve it up into little intellectual nuggets to be studied below a microscope. Be spontaneous…natural.'

'*Natural*?' Ella hissed at him tempestuously. 'This is the most unnatural thing I've ever done!'

His blue-shadowed jawline clenched. 'Only because you're fighting everything I make you feel.'

That he recognised her struggle, ineffective though it was, shook Ella, for it had not occurred to her that he might understand her that well. His impatience unconcealed, he dumped her down on the bed. 'This is sex', he had said with a detachment that ran contrary to her every instinct. But if their arrangement was to work, she reasoned, she had to stop judging him and wanting and expecting more than he was ever likely to give her. She had passed the last deadline: it was crunch time.

'How many guys did you say?' Aristandros enquired silkily, watching her shimmy beneath the sheet until only her shoulders could be seen.

Ella sat up, delicate facial bones tightening defensively. 'I *didn't* say!'

The silence stretched. A sardonic edge to his expressive mouth, Aristandros undressed, taking his time, every movement fluid with a grace that caught her eye no matter how hard she tried to avoid that side of the room. From the whipcord muscles of his shoulders to his beautifully defined torso, he was a vision of sculpted masculine perfection. He was also very well endowed and fully aroused, she could not help noticing. Her mouth ran dry and her heart began to pound.

'Less than fifty?' Aristandros asked casually.

Ella shot him an aghast glance.

'Definitely less than fifty,' he decided for himself.

'It's none of your damned business!' Ella launched back at him furiously. 'Stop making a production out of it!'

'Come out from below the sheet.'

In a series of violent movements, Ella kicked off the sheet and reclined back against the pillows in the exaggerated pose of a glamour model, with her spine arched to thrust out her chest. 'Satisfied?'

Aristandros raked his appreciative gaze over the voluptuous swell of her breasts in the turquoise bra. 'Not yet. Take it all off, *glikia mou.*'

Her blue-as-sapphire eyes rounded. '*Everything*?'

Aristandros inclined his handsome head in a confirmation that was a clear challenge. For a split second, Ella was rigid with rejection, and then she scrambled off the bed. Taking up a defiant stance, she peeled off her bra and discarded her knickers.

His attention nailed to her, dark eyes flaring hungrily over her pale, slender curves, Aristandros strode forward and snatched her up into his arms. 'I already feel like I waited a lifetime for you!' he growled, claiming her soft mouth with savage possessiveness even while his hands moulded to the pert mounds of her breasts and kneaded the swollen pink tips between his fingers.

Her body came alive with almost painful immediacy. Needles of bittersweet longing arrowed from her breasts to her pelvis, and awakened a hollow feeling that was swiftly followed by a sharp stab of desire that made her tummy muscles contract. His mouth on hers suddenly became a fierce necessity. The pressure of his hard, masculine lips and the erotic exploration of his tongue went some way towards satisfying the craving taking charge of her. The stimulating passage of his hands over her sensitised body made her push against the unyielding contours of his hard muscular torso. He backed her down on to the bed. Heat and restlessness had entered her bloodstream. All of a sudden she was alight with a need that she had known only once before. Then, as now, the power of that sexual hunger scared her with its unnerving strength. Of their own volition it seemed, however, that her hips lifted and her thighs eased apart, seeking ever more intimate contact with him.

Aristandros lifted his tousled head to look down at her, his smouldering gaze scanning her flushed cheeks and the swollen contours of her mouth. 'You'll enjoy yourself much more when you let go of that rigid self-control—'

'Don't taunt me,' Ella warned him grittily.

'I wasn't.' He frowned. 'I want this to be an unforgettable night.'

Her body a playground of tingling, energised responses, all of which seemed beyond her control, Ella shivered, so wound up with tension that it was an achievement just to think. She registered that this was Ari, the ultimate alpha male at his most driven, and seemingly sex was not quite as casual an event as he had made it sound. Even between the sheets he was set on scoring the highest possible results. At the same time, he was so beautiful that just looking at him turned her heart over. He shifted, the hair-roughened skin of his chest scratching against her jutting nipples and sending a scorching dart of extreme awareness down to the swollen heat and moisture at the very heart of her. In a movement that was utterly instinctive, she sank her fingers into his luxuriant black hair to drag him down to her and urge his mouth back onto hers again. He dealt her a frank look of surprise.

'You talk too much,' Ella told him baldly.

Laughter rumbled in his chest and then he kissed her. Complaint was the last thing on her mind, for in that department he had no equal. He kissed with an unholy passion. The all-encompassing hunger surged again and she clung to him, excitement taking over and overwhelming her final defences.

'*Se thelo*…I want you,' he bit out, studying her with dark-golden eyes that smouldered with appreciation. 'When you respond like this to me, it blows my mind, *khriso mou*.'

She writhed in whimpering reaction while he explored the slick, wet flesh between her thighs. She was so tender and he was so skilled that both stillness and silence were impossible for her. Sensation engulfed her with exquisite pleasure as he teased the tiny bud below the pale curls screening her feminine mound. All restraint was gone. Her entire being was centred on the throbbing need he had awakened and the wickedly tormenting expertise of his technique. The yearning hunger got stronger and stronger until it felt as though her whole body was primed on a knife-edge of intolerable tension and longing. When he finally tipped her off that edge into climax, it was as if an explosion began low in her pelvis and slowly, wonderfully, roared in wave after glorious wave through the rest of her.

She was still awash with wondering bliss and stunned by the intensity of the experience when Aristandros slid between her thighs and sunk his hands below her hips to raise her. His iron-hard shaft probed her lush opening, and she gasped at the strangeness of a sensation magnified by the incredible sensitivity of her tender flesh. He attempted to plunge deeper, but for an instant her body seemed to resist him. With a stifled exclamation he tipped back her knees to ease his entry. Her untried feminine sheath finally stretched to accommodate him, and she cried out at the sudden shockingly sensual pleasure of his penetration. Her heart was racing as he delved deeper into her, and she arched up, on fire with excitement and renewed hunger. Nothing had ever felt so amazing. She was spellbound by the heady exhilaration of his masculine dominance and the extraordinary pleasure that was building inside her again. Just moments later she surged feverishly to another sexual peak which shattered her like glass into a hundred glittering pieces and flung her into the sun. Stunned by the explosive intensity of the pleasure, she was better prepared when it happened yet again, before he achieved his own release.

In the aftermath of that wild rollercoaster experience, Ella was in shock and as physically weak as a newborn kitten, drained by her own extravagant response.

'My every dream comes true,' Aristandros purred as he stretched like a jungle cat in the heat of the sun. Rolling back to her, he dropped a kiss on her brow and studied her with unashamed satisfaction. 'A multi-orgasmic woman who sets my bed on fire, *khriso mou.*'

Ella was hugely embarrassed at having been so wildly responsive. She could not deny that sex with him had proved to be an extremely pleasurable activity. But, whether it was fair or otherwise, she pretty much hated him for the fact that he had made her enjoy herself. Her lovely flushed face bleak as a wintry day, she evaded his keen scrutiny because she felt she had let herself down. After all, she had planned just to tolerate his love-making, not leave him with the impression that he was an amazing lover.

'And so beautiful,' Aristandros remarked, trailing caressing brown fingers lazily through the silken tangle of white-blonde hair lying across her slim shoulder. 'But remarkably inventive with the truth.'

Her hackles rose instantly. Given the excuse, she pulled away from him and snapped, 'Meaning?'

'You said you'd had a lot of lovers. But I don't think there was even one.'

'Well, you'd be wrong!' she hissed furiously.

Aristandros captured her hand to imprison her when she began scrambling out of the other side of the bed. 'I've never shared a bed with a virgin before, but you felt as tight as one,' he imparted softly.

Affronted by the intimacy of that comment, Ella wrenched her hand out of his. 'Wishful thinking, eh?' she jibed, high spots of colour burning over her cheekbones. 'You're Greek to your backbone, aren't you? You've slept with scores of women but you don't want one who's enjoyed the same freedom. In fact, your ultimate hypocritical fantasy is a virgin!'

'Don't speak to me like that,' Aristandros intoned with an icy bite to his words.

'*Se miso*; I hate you!' Ella spat at him.

Stalking across the bedroom, Ella took refuge in the bathroom. She was trembling and her eyes were scratchy with the tears she was fighting back. He had become her first lover, but she would sooner have cut out her tongue than admit that fact to him. She didn't want to give him that satisfaction—the knowledge that she hadn't got really close to any man since he had walked out of her life seven years earlier, telling her that she would regret turning him down until her dying day. She had met other men, but sadly nobody who had had the same effect on her as Aristandros Xenakis. Having loved and lost him, she had been determined not to settle for anything less. And those high standards had ensured she'd stayed single and alone.

Recognising just how far she had now fallen from her own ideals hurt. Ari made her feel vulnerable and threatened. She already felt as though he had turned her inside out. She got into the shower to freshen up, still shaken that he should have noticed that she was something less than experienced. After years of athletic activity and the egg-donation process that had resulted in her sister conceiving, Ella had been confident that he would have no reason to ever guess the truth. Her pride utterly denied him any right to that truth.

She was wrapped in a towel when a knock sounded on the door. She flung it open. 'What now?'

'What's the matter with you?' Aristandros demanded rawly. 'We're good together. Tomorrow you meet Callie. What's wrong?'

The sound of her niece's name, the tacit reminder of their agreement, steadied Ella. 'Nothing's wrong. It's been a long day, and I suppose I'm tired,' she muttered, sidestepping him to leave the bathroom.

In the dressing room she selected a strappy night-dress and got back into bed, scolding herself for her loss of temper and control. She was being stupid. Antagonising Aristandros was pure insanity. Bitten, he would bite back, and she had the most to lose. She was not necessary to him and far from irreplaceable. Any number of women would be happy to assume the role of mistress, and none of them was likely to shout at him or insult him. He wasn't accustomed to that kind of treatment and he wouldn't tolerate it.

At dawn the following morning, she listened while Aristandros showered and dressed and left the room before she drifted off to sleep again. A maid wakened her a couple of hours later and told her that Aristandros would breakfast with her when she was ready. Aware that within a few hours at most she would be meeting Callie, Ella leapt out of bed with enthusiasm and rushed to get dressed. Breathless and unbelievably tense, she entered the elegant modern dining-room.

'Good morning,' she breathed stiltedly, every skin cell in her body jumping as Aristandros cast down his copy of the *Financial Times* and rose to his full, commanding height.

Having sex with him had increased her awareness by a factor of at least a hundred. Uneasily conscious of the intimate ache between her thighs and the still-swollen contours of her mouth, she felt the hot blood of embarrassment engulf her face with uncomfortable warmth even before she met his brilliant dark-golden eyes. He gave her a steady look that betrayed nothing beyond his rock-solid assurance and cool.

For some reason she remembered their first date seven years back, when he had wakened her whole family by arriving unannounced at an early hour to take her out sailing on his yacht. Her stepfather, had fawned on him to a mortifying degree while her twin half-brothers had hovered, unsure whether to approve or disapprove of a mega-rich Xenakis with a bad reputation taking an interest in one of their sisters. Only her mother had had reservations. Ella hadn't really appreciated just how rich, powerful and well-known Aristandros was until she saw the way other people treated him.

She was surprised by how much of an appetite she had, and she ate a good breakfast before asking tautly, 'Is Callie on her way here?'

'No. She'll be waiting for us on *Hellenic Lady* with her nurse. We're sailing home to Greece,' Aristandros informed her.

Like all of his family, Aristandros was never happier

than when he was on a boat. Susie had complained bitterly about Timon's love of the water, which she had not shared.

'I hope she likes me,' Ella muttered before she could think better of revealing that admission of insecurity.

'Of course she will.' Aristandros shot her a lingering look redolent of very male appreciation.

Her cheeks warming, Ella stirred her coffee.

'She's also very lucky I let you get out of bed this morning,' he husked.

Ella dealt him a startled glance from her vivid blue eyes.

Aristandros rested a lean-fingered brown hand on her slim thigh and urged her round to face him. 'I wanted to keep you awake all night. Moderation isn't my style, *koukla mou*.'

Wildly conscious of the unashamed hunger that had flared like liquid gold in his intense gaze, Ella found herself leaning forward to speed up the meeting of her mouth with his. She could not have explained what prompted her to make that encouraging move. But that spontaneous kiss was indescribably sweet and intoxicating, and it sent every nerve-ending jumping with vibrant energy and response. A quickening sensation thrummed low in her pelvis. A moment later, his hand was meshed in her hair, holding her to him, and a moment after that he had lifted her right out of the chair into his arms. Excitement blazed through her like solar flares as he carried her back to the bedroom…

CHAPTER FIVE

ELLA was so taut with anticipation that her heart almost leapt out of her chest when she first saw Callie in the reception salon of the Xenakis yacht.

At a glance she recognised how much her biological child resembled her, with that silvery-blonde cap of hair and those almond-shaped blue eyes. She wondered with painful regret if ironically that pronounced similarity had unleashed Susie's insecurity over her role as Callie's mother. The little girl straightened up to turn away from the toy she was playing with and focused not on Ella but on Aristandros. But, instead of toddling forward to greet the tall Greek as Ella expected, Callie waved at him and smiled. Aristandros waved back.

'She always smiles when she sees me,' Aristandros commented, evidently content with the style of his greeting.

Ella went over to meet her niece and got down on her knees, her heart lurching as she studied the child, whose very blue eyes were curious. A shy little hand reached out to touch Ella's equally pale hair and then hastily withdrew again. Recognising Callie's fear of the unfamiliar, Ella began talking to introduce herself, and within minutes totally forgot the presence of Aristandros and the Greek nursemaid stationed on the other side of the vast salon. When she recalled their presence she looked back over there but Aristandros had gone.

She soon discovered that Callie lit up when she heard music and loved to dance. The little girl giggled in delight when Ella joined in, and the atmosphere became much more relaxed. When refreshments were served, Ella sat down to get acquainted with her niece's youthful nurse, Kasma, and find out about the child's routine. While the two women talked, Ella made a hat out of a napkin to amuse Callie, who was becoming fractious. Callie finally consented to sit on Ella's lap to enjoy a fruit snack. Momentarily the warm, solid baby weight of the toddler resting trustingly against her made happy tears wash the back of Ella's eyes; this was a moment that she had truly believed she would never know in reality. Just then, every sacrifice she had made seemed more than worthwhile.

Kasma had a good deal to tell her that was of interest. The young woman stood in too much awe of Aristandros even to imply criticism of her employer. Even so, what Ella learned from subtle questions soon convinced Ella that Aristandros had zero parenting skills and, quite possibly, no interest in rectifying that deficiency. By then Callie was fast asleep in her arms, and Ella followed Kasma down to the lower-deck cabin which was set up as a nursery and put her niece in her cot for a nap.

Keen to freshen up—something Ella hadn't had a chance to do earlier that day after their rushed late departure from the London penthouse—she returned to the main cabin suite, where she took a shower in the superb marble wet-room. She couldn't stop smiling as she relived the afternoon that had just passed. The hours had just melted away while she'd been with Callie. A stewardess came to tell her that Aristandros was waiting for her in the salon. Ella finished drying her hair, her body tingling in outrageous tune with her thoughts, because she could not forget the pure, erotic excitement of Aristandros's love-making at the outset of the day, or the blissful release she had once again experienced in his arms.

'A change of plan—we're flying to Paris in an hour,' Aristandros announced when she joined him.

'Paris?' Her eyes homed in on him straight away and involuntarily clung to his compellingly handsome features. Even in the formal garb of a black pinstripe business-suit and dark silk tie, he emanated a charge of raw sexuality and animal energy that made her mouth run dry as a bone. 'Why?'

'Some friends are having a party, and I'm looking forward to showing you off.'

'But Callie's in bed and exhausted. She's just flown in from Greece,' Ella reminded him uncomfortably.

'She can sleep during the flight.' Aristandros shrugged, instantly dismissing her protest. 'Children are very resilient. I must have travelled round the world with my parents a score of times by her age. How did you get on with her?'

'We got on great, but it'll take time for her to bond with me.'

'You'll still be a better mother than Susie ever was,' Aristandros forecast with a hint of derision.

Astonishment and annoyance at that criticism flared through Ella in defence of her late sister. 'What on earth makes you say that?'

Engaged in flicking through a business file, Aristandros raised a sleek ebony brow and glanced up again. 'I'm not afraid of the truth, and death doesn't purchase sainthood. You should never have agreed to your sister's request that you donate eggs to enable her to become pregnant. Susie couldn't handle it. An anonymous donor would have been a safer bet.'

'What are you talking about?' Ella demanded angrily.

Aristandros dealt her an impatient look. 'Don't tell me that you never realised that as far as Susie was concerned you were the kid sister from hell? You outshone her in looks and intelligence, and compounded your sins by attracting my interest.'

'That's complete nonsense!'

'It's not. Susie tried to lure me long before she ever looked at Timon, but I didn't bite.'

Ella was shattered by a piece of information that had never come her way before. Susie had been attracted to Aristandros? That possibility, that very private and dangerous little fact, had never once occurred to her. 'Is that honestly the truth?'

Aristandros frowned. 'Why would I lie about it? I wasn't pleased when Susie started dating Timon, but he fell hook, line and sinker for her.'

Ella had lost colour, the fine bones of her profile prominent below her creamy skin. All of a sudden things that she had not understood but which had given her an uneasy feeling were being explained—her sister's constant, tactless carping about Ari's inability to stay faithful throughout the period when Ella had been seeing him; her repeated angry accusations that Ella didn't appreciate just how lucky she was.

'No matter what your sister did, Timon forgave her because he loved her. But, when you made it possible for them to have a child together and Susie turned her back on that child, Timon couldn't accept it.'

Ella gave him a stricken appraisal. 'Susie turned her back on Callie? How?'

'She left their staff to take care of her. Having got the baby she insisted she could not live without, she rejected her. Timon was at his wit's end. He consulted doctors on her behalf. Susie refused to see them, and finally Timon began to talk about divorcing Susie and applying for sole custody of Callie. Their marriage was very much on the rocks when they died.'

Her consternation and sadness at that news palpable, Ella sank heavily down on a chair. 'I had no idea that the situation was so serious. If only I had known, if only Susie had been willing to see me and talk to me after Callie's birth, maybe *I* could have—'

'You were the last person who could have helped her. She was too jealous of you.'

'It's perfectly possible that Susie was suffering from severe post-natal depression. Didn't my family try to help her?' Ella prompted feverishly.

'I don't think they recognised the extent of the problem, or that they wanted to get involved once they realised that Susie's marriage was in grave trouble,' Aristandros said flatly.

Ella knew that in such circumstances her domineering stepfather would have urged her mother to mind her own business, and that her mother would not have had the backbone to stand up to him even if she'd disagreed. She felt unbearably sad. Had Susie been suffering from depression? Evidently, however, even Timon had been unable to persuade her sibling to seek professional help. Poor Callie had had a troubled and insecure life right from the moment of her birth. Ella thought that it was hardly surprising that the little girl was quiet and somewhat behind in her development.

'How much time have you spent with Callie?' Ella asked Aristandros.

His well-defined black brows pleated, as if he suspected a trick question. 'I see her every day that we're under the same roof.'

'But do you play with her? Talk to her? *Hold* her?'

Aristandros winced at those blunt questions. 'I'm not a touchy-feely guy. That's what you're here for.'

Ella breathed in deep and stood up. 'I don't want to offend you, but I have to be frank. At the moment, all you seem to do is wave at her from the doorway of her nursery once or twice a day.'

Aristandros frowned and threw up his hands in objection at her censorious tone. 'It's a little game we play. What harm does it do?'

Ella was hanging on to her temper only by a hair's breadth. He was not that obtuse. He could hardly believe that he was playing father of the year with a long-distance wave. 'Callie needs to be touched and talked to and played with. The reason she didn't rush to greet you today is because you've got her accustomed to only seeing you at a distance—and that's how you like it, isn't it? Hands-off parenting? But she needs real contact with you—'

'What am I supposed to do with a baby?' Lean, strong face hard with impatience and hauteur, Aristandros ground out that demand, clearly offended by her criticism. 'I'm a very busy man and I'm doing my best.'

'I know you are. You just need a little direction,' Ella murmured, suddenly wondering if the closest he had ever got to his own dysfunctional parents was a breezy, noncommittal wave from the nursery door. 'And then you'd be brilliant, because you always do well at anything you set out to do.'

His dark eyes gleamed at that assurance while a wicked slow-burning smile tilted his beautiful mouth. 'Flattery will get you nowhere, *glikia mou*.'

'Will you think again about flying to Paris—for Callie's sake?' Ella pressed softly.

'You don't do sweet and submissive well.'

Mortified by the derisive tone that let her know that he had seen straight through her attempt to talk him round to her way of thinking, Ella stood straight as a blade, colour burnishing her cheeks. 'I was trying to be tactful.'

'I don't like it. It doesn't suit you,' Aristandros spelt out without skipping a beat. 'On the very first day you meet Callie, do I need to remind you that I make all the decisions where she's concerned?'

Ella turned very pale at that blunt reminder. She met cold eyes, the warning look of a strong male who had no intention of allowing his authority to be challenged. Her tummy flipped. He made her appreciate all over again that he was the one in control, and that she was walking a dangerous path from which she could not afford to stray. It was clear that he intended to hold her to the very letter of the agreement he had made her sign. She had promised not to interfere in Callie's up-bringing. All of a sudden she was appreciating just how difficult it was likely to be to take care of Callie while following his rules.

'*We* come first in this instance, not the child. *Don't* let her come between us and cause discord,' Aristandros advised her with forbidding emphasis.

Ella wanted to tell him how selfish and unreasonable he was being, but he had just delineated her boundaries as a warning and she did not dare. Aristandros Xenakis had spent thirty-two years on the earth doing exactly what he liked at all times. She might try to guide, but he would never allow her to lead. Who was she to think she could change him? The chill in the atmosphere raised gooseflesh on her bare arms and she turned to leave.

'Where are you going?'

Her spine prickled with apprehension. 'I, er, need to work out what I'm going to wear this evening.'

'No need. As yet you don't have a proper wardrobe. My staff will organise a selection of dresses to be brought to my Paris home for you, and your maid will do your packing. There's very little that you need to do for yourself now.'

Ella flipped back round. 'Sometimes you scare me…' And the instant she voiced that admission she regretted it, but there it was: the complete unvarnished truth.

Aristandros cast aside the file and vaulted upright. His astute eyes were unreadable, his fabulous bone-structure taut. 'I don't want that.'

Ella pinned her tremulous lips closed. 'I can't help the way I feel.'

'You're one of the strongest women I've ever known,' Aristandros countered.

But he was making a coward of her because if she spoke her mind she stood to lose too much, Ella conceded bitterly. Aristandros closed a hand over hers and tugged her closer. With an imperious shift of his handsome head, he smoothed her fingers straight and linked their hands. 'If it's that important, I'll make more effort with Callie.' Unusually he hesitated, his wide, sensual mouth compressing. 'I don't know how to go about it, though. I didn't have a conventional childhood.'

Ella was well aware that even that minor admission of ignorance was a major step for him, and that any sort of change of heart on his part was to be warmly appreciated and encouraged, but she was still so tense and worked up that her hand trembled in his. 'I *know*,' she said feelingly, her heart lurching inside her, for his cruelly troubled childhood had been lived out in the full glare of the media spotlight thanks to his larger-than-life parents and was very well documented.

'My earliest memory is of my father shouting at my mother when I almost drowned in a swimming pool. They were either drunk or high…' A broad shoulder shifted, his strong face hardening. 'They were so busy fighting they left me out on the terrace and forgot about me again. I know what *not* to do if you have a child.'

'Yes, of course you do,' she agreed. 'When you're a kid it's so frightening when you see adults fighting and out of control. The first time I saw Theo hit my mother, I thought the world was going to end…' As Ella realised what she had inadvertently revealed, she was appalled by her carelessness, and she fell silent.

'Repeat that,' Aristandros urged, his narrowed gaze reflecting his stunned reaction. 'The first time you saw your stepfather *hit* your mother?'

Ella was aghast at what she had let drop. 'I don't want to talk about it. I really didn't mean to say that!'

Aristandros lifted a hand to tip up her chin so that her eyes were forced to meet his. 'But now that you have, there's no going back or denying it. Theo Sardelos is in the habit of hitting your mother?'

Ella was pale as death, and full of the shame she had never been able to shake over that sordid reality. 'I don't think the violence happens as much now as it once did…at least, I would hope not,' she confided jerkily. 'But it's been so long since I had any contact with them, I really have no idea.'

'Did he ever hit *you*?' Aristandros growled.

'No, only my mother. It's a pity he didn't have a legal agreement drawn up like you did before they got married, though I'm not sure she would have signed up if she'd known what she was in for!'

'What the hell are you saying?' Aristandros grated.

'Well, that's why he beat her up—she objected when he didn't come home at night. He was always with other women,' Ella explained grudgingly. 'I think he had affairs with every secretary he ever had, as well as with some of the friends Mum made over the years. Like you, he's very attractive to the opposite sex and an incorrigible womaniser.'

Brilliant dark eyes assailed hers with cold, hostile force. 'I've never hurt a woman in my life, nor would I.'

'I didn't insinuate that you would. That's not why you scare me,' Ella extended tightly. 'You scare me because you're so cold-blooded, so tough and determined to win every bout. It's your way or the highway, and trying not to fall foul of that is a constant challenge.'

'I don't want you to feel like that, but I can't change what I am.' Aristandros breathed, with a raw edge to his deep drawl. 'The fact you compared me to Theo Sardelos is revealing. You see us as similar personalities, a comparison which I absolutely reject. But I *am* shocked by what I have just learned. I can hardly credit that you never breathed a word to me about what was going on in your own home seven years ago.'

'It was a private matter. I grew up with a mother who swore me and my siblings to silence. We were brought up to be ashamed of it and keep it hidden. The violence was never, ever discussed. Everybody tried to pretend it didn't happen.'

'Even your brothers?' Aristandros prompted with growing incredulity. 'Susie never mentioned it to Timon either.'

'Susie just ignored it, and the twins were still quite young when I left home to go to university. I don't know how things stand now. I've always hoped it stopped, but I suspect that was rather foolish wishful thinking,' she muttered heavily. 'Look, can we please drop this subject?'

Unsympathetic to that plea, Aristandros settled his smouldering gaze on her. 'You thought I might be like your stepfather, didn't you? That's one of the reasons you wouldn't marry me.'

'I don't want to discuss this any more,' Ella told him quietly, and she turned on her heel and simply walked out of the salon. She was shaking like a leaf and cursing her unwary tongue. There was no way she could tell him the truth. Of course she had seen a similarity between him and her stepfather. But with Aristandros it had not been violence she feared, but the terrible pain, constant fear and suspicion of living with an unfaithful partner. She had loved him too much to face that prospect.

Ella was overseeing her packing when Aristandros strode into the state room. With a casual movement of one hand he dismissed the maid while wrenching off his tie with the other. 'You've kept too many secrets from me, *moli mou*,' he delivered harshly. 'I don't like that. I will tell you now—that *has* to change.'

Ella slanted a feathery brow. 'Just like that?'

Inflexible dark-golden eyes clashed with her defiant gaze. 'Just like that. Don't try to keep me out of the loop.'

'Ari...threats and warnings don't create the kind of atmosphere that encourages trust and the sharing of confidences,' Ella countered, the flush on her cheek-bones accentuating the sapphire brightness of her eyes.

Aristandros shrugged off his jacket. 'Exactly when were you planning to tell me that you have had no contact with your family for years?'

Ella stiffened. 'I already told you that when I admitted that nobody contacted me to tell me that Susie and Timon had died. There was a huge row the night I said I wouldn't marry you. I haven't seen my family since then.'

Aristandros frowned. 'The rift developed that far back?'

'Yes. As far as Theo was concerned, it was my duty to marry you for the good of the family. He was livid. My brothers thought I was insane to say no, as well. They took your side, not mine, because you're filthy rich and a profitable business connection and I'm not,' she advanced bitterly. 'If it had happened a couple of centuries ago, they would have cheerfully locked me up in a convent and left me there to rot for the rest of my life!'

'I didn't know your family had reacted that strongly. Timon did mention that you didn't come home any more, but I assumed that that was because you were too busy with your training,' Aristandros admitted. 'Now that you're with me and Callie, they can hardly continue to behave as if you don't exist.'

'Don't you believe it. I don't get on with Theo. I never did.'

'You don't need to get on with him or anyone else you dislike now,' Aristandros informed her lazily. 'My guest lists are extremely select.'

Ella tried not to think of her stepfather's rage if he found himself suddenly excluded from the Xenakis social circle, and stilled a shiver. She watched Ari peel off his shirt to reveal the rugged musculature of his powerful chest and flat, hard stomach. He really did have the most beautiful body, she acknowledged helplessly. Her nipples tightened into taut, swollen buds beneath her bra. A clenching tight sensation between her thighs made her tense. She was remembering the smooth, steely heat of his skin when she touched him, the tormentingly sexy slide of his strong, hard body against hers. The palms of her hands prickled. The tender flesh at the heart of her throbbed with awareness.

Aristandros surveyed her with a sardonic amusement that was shockingly aware. 'No,' he breathed. 'We haven't got the time. Pleasure is all the sweeter when deferred, *glikia mou*.'

When Ella registered that he had realised just how

she was feeling at that moment, she boiled alive with embarrassment and self-loathing. Did she really find him that irresistible? How could her body get so out of step with her pride that it betrayed her? Was she really such a sexual pushover that she could hardly wait for him to touch her again? Could the experience of physical pleasure change her so much, or make her feel so disgustingly *needy*? Ella stifled an inner shudder of distaste at that image. What was happening to her? All of a sudden she felt like a hormonal teenager suffering from an embarrassing crush that had got out of control.

Callie began crying at the airport. Over-tired and rudely awakened from her rest, the little girl was in no mood to find herself in strange places surrounded by unfamiliar faces and voices. By the time the Xenakis private jet took off, Callie was fully wound up and screaming at the top of her lusty lungs. Without a word, Ella went to assist Kasma, who was looking distinctly frazzled round the edges when Callie continued to sob in spite of all her efforts to the contrary.

'This is a nightmare. Mr Xenakis is being disturbed,' the young nursemaid said guiltily to Ella. 'That should never happen.'

Ella soon discovered that there was no magic solution capable of quickly settling an exhausted and very cross toddler who was merely expressing her distress at having her settled routine destroyed. Although Callie could be distracted for a few minutes, she would soon start grizzling again. Ella took her into the sleeping compartment, sat down on the bed and rocked and sang to the little girl. Miraculously that seemed to calm Callie down, but she then objected vociferously to Ella's every attempt to put her down again. Ella took charge of her for the flight.

'Give her back to her nurse,' Aristandros instructed when they were about to board the waiting pair of limousines in Paris.

Callie tried to cling and had to be prised off Ella, a process which caused sobs to break out again. Ella found it very hard to walk away.

'Well, I don't think we need to worry about the bonding process,' Aristandros remarked with an outstanding lack of tact and sympathy. 'You're clearly a whiz in the maternal stakes. It's only day one and Callie's already doing a great impression of a limpet.'

'She's upset,' Ella fielded tightly.

'One of life's lessons is that she can't always have you when she wants you,' Aristandros countered. 'For what is left of the afternoon you will be fully occupied.'

Indeed, Ella barely had time to catch her breath at his magnificent Paris townhouse before a parade of breathtaking evening gowns arrived for her perusal. A phalanx of beauticians followed to groom her for the party. This time Ella was less tolerant of the beauty regime imposed on her. Indeed, because she would have much preferred to spend time with Callie, she fretted through every step of having her nails, hair and make-up brought to a glossy standard of perfection that she could never have achieved for herself. A maid helped her into the rich blue dress she had picked to wear, and she surveyed her reflection. Her silvery-fair hair fell in a sleek curtain round her shoulders, the designer dress a wonderful frame for her tall, slender

figure. Acknowledging that she had never looked so
good in her life before, however, had no impact on her
frustration at the prospect of having to go through the
same prolonged beauty routine every time she went
out in public.

Aristandros strode through the door. 'I want you to
wear this set.'

Hugely conscious of his appraisal, Ella lifted the
large jewel-case he had tossed down on the bed. As she
lifted the lid on a magnificent sapphire-and-diamond
necklace and earrings, she gasped. 'My goodness…I'm
impressed.'

'So you should be. It's a family set.'

Ella tensed. 'Then I shouldn't be wearing it.'

'They've been mouldering in a safe for decades.
Someone might as well wear them,' Aristandros de-
creed in a bored tone that strangled the further protest
on her tongue.

Feeling more than ever like a doll being decked out
in decorative trappings, Ella put on the jewels. 'I want
to check on Callie before we leave,' she told him then,
barely glancing in the mirror to see how the superb
necklace and earrings became her.

'You have five minutes.'

Ella was dismayed to discover that her niece was
still awake and crying intermittently. She had also
pushed away the food that Kasma had tried to give her.
Ella lifted the little girl out of her cot and examined her.
She soon discovered that Callie was running a temperature and had swollen lymph-glands in her neck.

'What's wrong?' Aristandros demanded from behind
her a few minutes later.

'I think Callie has tonsillitis. It's probably viral, so antibiotics won't do any good.'

Aristandros turned to the PA hovering at his elbow and instructed him to arrange for a doctor to call. Ella worried at her lower lip. Callie was miserable, and Ella didn't want to leave her. Aristandros flashed her a sardonic look, and her chin came up at what she recognised as a direct challenge. She sped over to Kasma and hastily wrote down her mobile-phone number so that the nurse could keep her in touch with developments. She squeezed Callie's hot little hand and walked away with guilty tears burning her own eyes.

'She's not seriously ill, is she?' Aristandros breathed.

'No, of course she isn't. She'll be fine.'

'So, remember that you're a doctor and stop over-reacting,' Aristandros urged. 'We're going to a party.'

'I'd rather stay here,' Ella admitted, wondering how he was contriving to make her feel guilty as well. Her desire to comfort Callie had nothing whatsoever to do with her being a doctor.

'But another doctor will be checking her out. She is in the best of hands. If there is further cause for concern, we will be informed,' Aristandros pointed out levelly.

Feeling that she was making an unnecessary fuss, Ella breathed in slow and deep, and caught her reflection in a giant mirror as they descended the sweeping staircase into the hall. She barely recognised herself with the spectacular jewels glittering at her throat and ears, and the glorious dress shimmering in the soft lights.

Aristandros closed a hand over hers. 'You look gorgeous, *moli mou*.'

CHAPTER SIX

THE PARTY WAS BEING thrown by Thierry Ferrand, an international banker and one of Aristandros's closest friends. Thierry and his wife, Gabrielle, lived on the exclusive Avenue Montaigne near the Champs-Elysées, where a huge crowd of paparazzi was waiting on the street to catch photos of the guests arriving. This time round, Ella copied Aristandros, held her head high and acted as if the members of the press were invisible.

The Ferrand apartment had been transformed with jaw-dropping extravagance into a Moroccan backdrop for the party. The colourful tented walls, hanging lanterns and the hall fountain scattered with aromatic rose petals made Ella's eyes widen. Aristandros anchored her to his side and introduced her to their hosts. She took an immediate liking to Gabrielle, a lively brunette with a contagious smile.

'I believe you're a doctor?' Thierry Ferrand remarked.

'Yes, but I'm no longer practising,' Ella replied, a touch flatly.

Gabrielle studied her in surprise. 'But why not?'

'Ella plans to devote herself to my ward and her niece, Callie,' Aristandros advanced.

'It's not easy to settle into being a lady of leisure,' Gabrielle remarked. 'I'm a corporate lawyer, Ella, and by the time my maternity leave was over I was ready to *run* back to work!'

'You have a child?' Ella asked.

Gabrielle needed no further encouragement to part Ella from Aristandros and take her upstairs to show off her adorable ten-month-old daughter who was fast asleep in her cot. The two women chatted.

'You're so normal and natural, not Ari's usual style of companion,' Gabrielle commented, her curiosity unhidden. 'Several of his exes are here tonight, and the usual squad of man-hungry singles. I shouldn't have dragged you away from him. You can't afford to leave Ari alone for a moment. Women really do go mad for him.'

Ella shrugged, still bone-deep furious with Aristandros at his stony-hearted response to Callie's illness and his determination that Ella should leave her to attend the party. As far as Ella was concerned, at that moment any woman was welcome to him. 'Ari is very well able to look after himself,' she said lightly.

Her mobile phone rang before she rejoined Aristandros, and she stayed out in the hall where it was quieter to talk to Kasma. Callie was still miserable, thirsty, but refusing to drink because of her sore throat. Furthermore, her high temperature remained a source of concern. When Ella put her phone away she registered that Aristandros was watching her. He beckoned her with in an imperious gesture that brooked no refusal. Her full lips compressed; she felt like a disobedient dog having her choke-chain yanked.

Impervious to her mood, Aristandros ran an appreciative forefinger below the pouting line of her lower lip. 'You look like a queen tonight.'

Her bright-blue eyes gleamed. 'Worthy of your investment?'

'Only time will tell,' Aristandros traded in a typically oblique response. 'But you're definitely a trophy. Every man in the room has noticed you.'

'I'm thrilled,' Ella fenced in a bored monotone.

An appreciative glint lit his shrewd dark eyes, and smouldering sensuality curved his expressive mouth. 'Not now, but you will be later. I intend to make the most of the fact that you're mine to take home, *khriso mou*.'

With his security team acting as a protective filter, a constant flow of people tried to approach Aristandros. A few were friends, most were interested in talking business opportunities, but an equal number were chancers eager to take advantage of an opportunity to meet one of the richest men in the world. Ella, engaged in watching how other women reacted to him, was constantly amazed by how much blatant encouragement and flirtation came his way, even while she stood there right beside him. He introduced her to only a handful of people.

'Let's dance,' Aristandros urged, predictably getting bored with the social chitchat, and closing his hand over hers to extract her from the crush surrounding him at speed.

It was the first time in over an hour that he had even acknowledged her existence. They had barely reached the edge of the floor when Ella's mobile phone vibrated its call signal in her clutch bag. Extracting it in spite of Aristandros's exasperated scrutiny, she left him and returned to the hall to speak to Kasma.

She learned that the doctor had visited and confirmed Ella's diagnosis of tonsillitis and the treatment she had advised. The medication was finally kicking in to reduce Callie's fever and ease the pain of her sore throat. Lighter of heart, Ella went off in search of Aristandros, wondering whether he deserved to hear the good news or not.

Gabrielle intercepted her for a chat, and it was just after parting from her that Ella's phone rang yet again. Ella was astonished when she put the phone back to her ear and heard a voice she had truly believed she might never hear again.

'Ella…is that you?' Jane Sardelos was demanding. 'That friend of yours, Lily, gave me your number.'

'*Mum*?' Ella framed, dry-mouthed with shock, wandering restlessly over to a window and staring out sightlessly at the lights of Paris.

'Where are you?'

'I'm in Paris.'

'With *him*? I understand that there was a picture of you in a British newspaper with Aristandros Xenakis. I couldn't believe it was you, until it was confirmed. What are you doing with him?' her mother pressed feverishly.

'I'm living with him and helping to look after Callie,' Ella admitted with pronounced reluctance.

'Are you out of your mind? You wouldn't marry him when he asked you, but seven years on you're happy to be his whore?'

As that horrible word struck Ella like a physical blow, perspiration dampened her upper lip. 'It's not like that, Mum—'

'Of course it is. It couldn't be any other way with a Xenakis in a leading role. We're all disgusted and embarrassed by your behaviour. What do you think this does to our standing in the eyes of family and friends? How could you be so selfish? How could you shame us like this?'

'Morals have moved on for women since the Middle Ages,' Ella protested. 'I'm in a relationship with Aristandros. It doesn't mean I've become a whore.'

'Your stepfather says that, because of you, we won't be able to visit Callie now!' Jane Sardelos complained with a sob. 'He says that if we do it will look like we're condoning the situation.'

Ella was pale. 'That's untrue and unreasonable. You're Callie's grandmother, and your right to see her should not be influenced in any way by my relationship with Ari.'

'Every picture tells a story, Ella,' her mother interrupted bitterly. 'Only last month, Ari Xenakis was with another woman, one of a *very* long line of other women. Now, all of a sudden, you're wearing a designer dress and a fortune in diamonds round your throat that you could never have afforded to buy for yourself. So, tell me—if that doesn't make you a whore, what does?'

The phone went dead with wounding emphasis, denying Ella the chance to defend herself further. A little voice asked her wryly what more she could possibly have said when it was so clear that her parent wouldn't have been prepared to listen. Numb and sick inside, and with her mother's angry accusations still ringing in her ears, Ella replaced the phone in her clutch bag. A whore: it was not a word she had ever heard on her rather prim mother's lips before. But she knew who would have voiced that abusive word in the first instance: her stepfather. Theo would have stormed and shouted until his wife was upset enough to call her daughter and pass on the official family opinion personally. It would not have been the first time that Theo had used her mother as his mouthpiece.

Gabrielle Ferrand approached and addressed Ella with a strained look on her lovely face. 'I think you'd better go and rescue Ari before a catfight breaks out over him.'

Frowning and totally distracted after her upsetting phone call, Ella followed the brunette and saw Aristandros seated in a lazy sprawl across a sofa. Three gorgeous women literally had him surrounded. They were all over him like a rash, laughing and chattering and giving him looks, little touches and signals that were blatant sexual invitations. Ella felt nauseous just watching the scene, and she waited for Aristandros to take back his own space. If ever a guy had been born to look after himself without any help from anyone else, it was Aristandros. But he made no move to rebut the advances coming his way, and when one of the women sprang up he accompanied her on to the dance floor.

'He's been on his own almost all evening,' Gabrielle muttered frantically. 'He's not used to being neglected.'

'You're saying I've neglected him?' Ella queried while she watched Aristandros and a sexy redhead salsa-dancing with considerable dexterity and enjoyment. She hadn't even known he could move like that. Seeing him smile and allow his body to connect intimately with another woman's hurt like a knife cutting through tender skin. There was an enormous amount of flirtation going on. She was glued to the spot, trapped by ghoulish curiosity and tormented by more pain than she could have believed possible.

'I didn't mean to sound critical,' her companion retorted uncomfortably.

'Don't worry about it. Ari has more than his fair share of charisma. Women always make excuses for him when he behaves badly,' Ella commented, having met with that female reaction to Aristandros on many occasions seven years earlier. 'But I'm afraid I don't.'

Unfortunately, Aristandros was simply being himself—an unapologetic womaniser set on amusement. Ella, however, could not bear to have that fact paraded right under her nose, particularly when her mother's condemnation of their affair was stuck like a giant immoveable rock in the middle of her every thought and reaction. Surely only a woman worthy of the label 'whore' would stand by and just accept Ari's behaviour?

'I can't stay, Gabrielle. Will you tell Ari I've left? But don't rush to do it,' Ella advised, turning on her heel to move towards the front door.

'Don't do it, Ella. I really like you, and he'll be furious if you walk out on him,' the other woman protested. 'I'm sure you're right. He's only flirting…it means absolutely nothing to him. Women of that sort come onto him every day. But you're different, not least because you happen to be wearing the Xenakis sapphires and possess a brain.'

Ella glanced back at Aristandros and the redhead. She felt sick with rage and hurt, and the depth of her reaction terrified her. The hand she employed to push her hair off her hot, damp brow was trembling. She travelled down in the lift to the ground floor where the concierge called a taxi for her. Cameras flared as she departed alone and in considerably less state than she had arrived. By then she was willing to acknowledge that she was running away from her own feelings as much as she was turning her back on a scene of public humiliation. But she was horrified by her over-sensitivity and the powerful emotions churning around inside her. Why should it matter to her so much what Aristandros did? Wasn't she capable of switching off her emotional responses to him? Just then she didn't care about the agreement she had signed. She refused to act like some whore he owned and to do as he expected regardless of how he himself behaved. A dignified departure from the party was truly the only option she could live with.

Back at the townhouse she headed straight for the nursery. Callie was slumbering peacefully, while Kasma was also asleep in her bed in the next-door bedroom with the door ajar. Ella gazed down at the little girl with a volcanic mixture of relief, love and pain rocketing through her. She reminded herself that Callie had managed fine before she was around, and would scarcely miss her, and that while she stayed her mother would refuse to visit her granddaughter. How could she allow that to happen?

Her maid helped her remove the dress and the sapphires and brought her a case when she asked. Ella put on jeans and a T-shirt and packed the few personal items she had brought from London. Then the heavy thud of the front door reverberated through the whole house, and she went rigid.

'Ella!'

Ella gulped at the harsh sound of her name on Aristandros's lips. 'I'm up here…'

Aristandros filled the doorway, strong features taut, eyes blazing a challenge. 'What in hell are you playing at?'

Ella settled bright-blue eyes on him, her chin at a defiant angle. 'What were *you* playing at? If you think I'm going to stand around while you carry on with other women in front of me, you have another thought coming!'

'You don't walk out on me in a public place… *ever*!' Aristandros raked back at her in a tone of fierce condemnation.

'You can tear up the agreement. I'm leaving you, so all bets are off.'

'You're all grown-up now,' Aristandros lanced back with derision. 'You're not allowed to run away when things get too hot for you.'

'I've never run away from anything in my life!' Ella yelled back at him, her temper unleashing like a dam overflowing.

'You run from anything that upsets you.'

'I'm not upset!' Ella practically screamed at him.

'This is not the calm, sensible Ella that I know.'

'But you don't *know* me!'

A sleek ebony brow listed. 'Don't I?'

'No, you don't!' she repeated squarely.

Aristandros settled scornful dark eyes on her. 'I have to confess that I didn't expect quite such a hysterical reaction.'

'Who are you calling hysterical?' Ella threw the demand at him furiously. 'And why the use of that word, "expect"? Are you suggesting that you deliberately chose to flirt with other women to get a reaction out of me?'

His brooding gaze locked to her hectically flushed and lovely face, Aristandros spread brown hands in a graceful gesture that neither confirmed nor denied. 'Would I do something that calculating?'

'Yes!' Ella's seething gaze was glued to him, her accusing stance unabated. 'Yes, you would if it amused you, because you are the most naturally devious and manipulative man I have ever met.'

'I could simply have told you that you were behaving badly,' Aristandros sliced back. 'It's ill-mannered to keep on taking phone calls in company.'

Outraged by that censure of her own behaviour, Ella looked at him in raw disbelief. 'How *dare* you tell me that I was behaving badly?'

His sculpted jawline squared even more, and he settled his steady gaze on her with considerable cool. 'It's the truth. Your behaviour was atrocious this evening. You went out in a sulk and you never came out of it.'

'That's a ridiculous thing to say!'

'Is it? You didn't want to leave Callie.'

'So, I'm human and caring, which is more than anyone could say of your attitude tonight. You didn't give a damn that she was ill!' Ella condemned him hotly.

'Then why did I ensure that I spoke to the doctor who attended her? And why did I check back with Kasma after that?'

Ella ground her teeth together, while giving him a look that would have withered a lesser man. 'I didn't know you'd talked to the doctor…you didn't mention it.'

'In short, I was as informed as you were, with regard to your many phone conversations,' Aristandros skimmed back, smooth as glass.

An almost overwhelming desire to slap him threatened Ella's cracking composure. 'Maybe you did speak to the doctor.'

Aristandros dealt her a tough look. 'I'm not lying. I

may not get all emotional and dramatic like you do, but that doesn't mean that I wasn't also concerned about Callie tonight.'

In receipt of that cutting, hard-hitting reproof, Ella snatched in a deep, steadying breath. 'I apologise if I misjudged you on that score.'

'You did,' Aristandros drawled, rubbing salt in an already open wound.

'But I do not sulk…and I certainly wasn't sulking earlier!' Ella slung back at him angrily.

'Maybe you have another word for it, but you were definitely in a strop.'

'I was annoyed with you,' she admitted grudgingly.

'I'm not so thick-skinned that I didn't get the message, but it was juvenile to parade your mood in public.' Aristandros sent her a grim look. 'I'm a very private man and I value discretion, but tonight you made a scene for the gossip columns. Do it one more time and I'm sending you back to London.'

Ella sent him a fiery look of sheer loathing. 'You don't need to send me any place. I'm leaving. But, my word, you are good at turning the tables, You haven't said one word about your own inappropriate behaviour, except to imply that you were giving other women encouraging signals purely to rile me.'

Aristandros laughed out loud, the unexpected sound of his amusement shattering the tense atmosphere in the room. 'Not to rile you.'

'I don't give a damn what you do,' Ella hissed, slamming the case shut and closing it.

'Liar,' Aristandros framed silkily. 'For a woman who doesn't do jealousy, you were red-hot with it tonight.'

Ella went rigid, shot him a fuming appraisal and swung the case down. She was so mad she wanted to throw things at him. How dared he accuse her of being jealous? How dared he have the power to divine feelings she had not even admitted to herself? As she stalked across the room in a rage, he cut across her path and snatched the case off her. 'What the heck do you think you're doing?' she shouted at him.

'I'm preventing you from doing something very stupid, *moli mou*,' Aristandros growled, throwing open the door of the dressing room and slinging the case in there with a resounding crash.

'I'm not some whore who's going to take whatever you throw at her!' Ella flung at him wrathfully, adrenalin pumping like crazy through her veins and making it impossible for her to stay still or even think with any rationality. 'I'm not interested in your money or what you can buy me. I'm not impressed. Nothing you could give me would persuade me to tolerate the kind of treatment you gave me tonight!'

'Even if I admit that the only woman I want is you?' Aristandros chided, leaning elegantly back against the door to close it. 'Yes, I conducted an experiment tonight, I wanted a reaction.'

'An experiment?' Ella parrotted with raw incredulity.

'A harmless one. Only a very possessive woman would get so worked up at the sight of me dancing with another woman.'

Her slim hands clenched into fists. So much emotion was hurtling round inside her that she felt frighteningly violent, and yet terrifyingly vulnerable at the same time.

'But that's all that I did,' Aristandros continued steadily. 'Nothing else.'

The hard truth of that statement struck Ella like an avalanche powerful enough to knock her off her feet. So he had danced with another woman and smiled and laughed…big deal! Social interactions of that ilk were normal at parties. What had made her overreact to such an extent? Why did she feel like rage was ready to explode out of her because she couldn't contain it? He had wanted a reaction and she had given it to him. *Only a very possessive woman*… And in spite of all her denials she *was* possessive, wasn't she? Violently possessive, with feelings and responses born from years of sitting by on the sidelines looking at photos of Ari with other women and reading about his affairs. Lily had suggested it was an unhealthy obsession, and so it was, for it had fostered a bone-deep streak of jealousy that she had not even recognised for what it was.

'Maybe I overreacted.' Ella voiced those words as though they were composed in a foreign language she found hard to pronounce. It was an acknowledgement of folly which cost her pride dear. For a moment she was standing outside herself and wondering in horror at the raging mindless jealousy that had consumed her and almost persuaded her to burn every one of her boats. Had she truly been willing to sacrifice Callie in that conflagration as well? She was genuinely appalled.

The silence stretched, drawn tight by her strain.

Ella focused on Ari's lean, classic profile, her nervous tension at an incredible high. He had set her up to see how she would react to his flirtation, and he would have had to torture her to get an apology out of her. She hated him, not only for doing that to her, but also for appreciating that what he had made her feel scared her. Suddenly she did not want to probe the precise nature and cause of the madness that had overpowered her common sense. 'The last couple of days—all the changes in my life—have been an incredible strain,' she said instead, her low voice tight and stilted, because her pride was cringing at the excuse she was using.

'Of course,' Aristandros breathed with an almost instantaneous agreement of that explanation that took her aback.

She was standing beside a mirror, and she looked at herself. The illusion of perfection was gone now, replaced by tousled hair, smudged mascara, lipstick and a T-shirt bought at a rock concert.

'Sometimes I push too hard.' Aristandros murmured that concession without any expression at all. 'But don't ever walk out on me like that again.'

Ella jerked her head in agreement, her throat taut with self-restraint. He had pushed her so hard that he had almost broken her. She was scared that she was going to cry as her jangling emotions continued to surge without any hope of being vented. She was fighting to reinstate intelligence and control. He reached for her before she could seal shut the dangerous gaps in her mental armour. The intoxicating sensuality of his mouth met hers in a hot, melting collision.

She fell into that kiss like a drowning swimmer in search of air. Hunger exploded through her every nerve ending in a chain reaction. Her hands delved deep into his thick, black hair. She could feel the raw passion pent up in his powerful body, and even the clothing between them couldn't douse her awareness of the bold ridge of his erection. The sure knowledge of his desire made resisting her own need impossible. The taste of him went to her head, and she felt dizzy and breathless. He curved his hands to her hips and settled her on the side of the bed where he proceeded to dispense with the barrier of her jeans.

'I can't salsa dance like that,' Ella heard herself say abruptly. 'Like that redhead—'

'I can take care of that,' Aristandros declared, pushing up the T-shirt and burying his face in the scented valley between her high breasts, impatiently while he peeled her free of the expensive scraps of satin and lace that still separated him from her slender curves.

Her chest rose and fell rapidly with the short, straining breaths she drew. She was hyper-aware of his every move. The abrasive brush of his stubble against the smooth slope of her breasts sent a violent shiver through her. The scent of him that close left her liquid with longing. 'I want you,' she admitted in a driven undertone.

Lush black lashes lifted from scorching golden eyes. 'I have died and gone to heaven,' Aristandros breathed softly. 'I thought I was never going to hear those words from your lips.'

'We've only been together two days!' Ella protested.

'Since when have I had patience?' Aristandros traded, long fingers skating over the tormentingly tender flesh between her thighs with a provocative skill that caused a startled gasp to part the swollen contours of her lips.

Her head tipped back against the pillows and her spine incurved. A glorious, heavy lassitude was spreading through her limbs, closely followed by energising darts of erotic sensation. She strained up to him, moaning out loud when he used his sensual mouth to tease and taste her urgently sensitive nipples. There was a sweet, painful tightness gathering in her pelvis as her inner muscles tensed and her hips squirmed in a rhythmic pattern against the sheet. She wanted, *needed* him. He turned her over on to her stomach and raised her on to her knees.

For a split second Ella didn't know what he intended but, an instant later he plunged his fully engorged manhood into her yearning flesh. Shock and wild excitement gripped her in an overpowering wave. His every deep thrust sent a hot, primitive charge to electrify her. The erotic pleasure of his virile dominance ravished her sense, and she whimpered her delight, encouraging him with every yielding flex of her hips. The seething tension and disturbed emotions she had stored up were blown away by a spellbinding orgasm that flooded her body with ecstasy and drained her of energy.

'Better?' Aristandros muttered thickly, curving her into his arms in the dizzy, dreamy aftermath when she honestly felt that she would never move again.

'Still floating,' she whispered before she could think better of it.

He leant over her, keen dark eyes lustrous as polished jet beneath the fringe of his black lashes. 'So why do you fight me?'

Ella rested her head against a brown muscular shoulder, revelling in the intimate connection of their bodies and the gloriously familiar scent of his skin. 'I like a challenge?'

His incredibly handsome features taut, Aristandros closed his arms round her and studied her with sardonic force. 'Stop it now, *hara mou*. Making me angry is a bad idea.'

Ella let her fingers trail along the line of his ruthless but aesthetically beautiful mouth. 'It makes you more human, and no matter how hard I tried I couldn't ever be all giggly and flattering and submissive.'

'That's not what I want, either. Be natural, be yourself…the way you used to be without even trying,' Aristandros urged.

Ella lost colour and turned her head away, knowing there was no going back to the young woman he was remembering. Was that what he wanted from her—the impossible? The turning back of time? How could she be twenty-one years old again and in love for the first time in her life? Even thinking about being that vulnerable again turned her stone-cold with fear inside. Loving Ari again would be a one-way ticket to hell.

'If you stop looking for problems, you'll soon find that you can enjoy what we have,' Aristandros intoned with blistering conviction. 'We're sailing back to Greece tomorrow.'

But Ella was already recalling the crazy weeks when she had been twenty-one and madly in love with him. Everybody who was anybody had spent those weeks warning her that Ari Xenakis would quickly lose interest in her. That was his track record, and his appetite for beautiful women ensured that he had an intimidating reputation as a heartbreaker. Ella, however, remembered feeling ridiculously happy during that period. Cool reflection hadn't got a look-in. She had not continually rehashed their dates in her mind looking for hints that he might be considering a future with her, either, for that possibility had not even occurred to her. She had simply adored being with him and had lived for the moment.

He had taken her out sailing a lot, for long drives and lengthy meals, rarely inviting others to join them. They hadn't gone to many parties or clubs, and when they had they hadn't stayed long. They had talked constantly and she had been herself, for she had not known how to be anything else in those days. Hard as it was to credit now, she had believed she had met her soulmate in Ari. The second time she'd called a halt to their love-making he had just laughed and made no further attempt to persuade her into bed. When he'd invited her to his grandfather's seventy-fifth birthday celebrations, she'd been overjoyed, because she had known how close Drakon was to his grandson and had felt honoured to be invited to meet him.

Now, a good deal older and wiser, she lay in the darkness, dully, painfully, reliving that final evening.

'I love you,' Aristandros had told her squarely, and she had responded with the same words. And, although he had afterwards accused her of insincerity, she had really meant what she said.

'I want to be with you. Will you marry me?' he had asked.

And her heart had bounced as high as a rubber ball, since it had not occurred to her then that he might have made the offer with sacrificial restrictions attached, a sort of trick question which was likely to come back and haunt her and leave her heartbroken. She had dimly assumed that they would get engaged and that Ari would visit her in London and marry her once she had completed her training. When he had got up to make a speech in honour of his grandfather's birthday, he had announced their engagement—along with the news that she would be giving up medicine.

Reality had swiftly burst her bubble of happiness. After a ferocious argument he had dumped her, and minutes later retracted the announcement he had made. Her family had taken her home in disgrace, unable to believe or come to terms with the startling idea that she could possibly have refused to marry a Xenakis.

Aristandros catapulted her back into the present by hauling her up against his lithe, muscular frame. Blue eyes very wide, she clashed with his heavily lidded, smouldering, dark-golden gaze. This man, she acknowledged with a fast-beating heart, already had the power to make her feel bitterly jealous and act in an irrational way. He was dangerous, was a very dangerous threat in every way to her peace of mind.

'Once is not enough,' he growled sexily, half under his breath. 'I still want you, *moli mou*.'

And some very basic element in Ella exulted in her sexual hold over him. In that instant, her heart racing, her pulses quickening and her treacherous body quivering with anticipation, she was a slave to the promise of the pleasure he would give her and she had no time to spare for agonising over the label that other people might affix to her position in his life.

CHAPTER SEVEN

TEN days later, Hellenic Lady arrived in Athens.

Ella was still in bed in the yacht's magnificent main state-room and she was devouring the British newspapers, several of which contained items about her. It was an extraordinary experience to suddenly see herself appear for the first time in print in the guise of a celebrity. In her case, however, her fame was purely borrowed from association with Aristandros. She was variously described as his 'new companion, Dr Dazzler', 'Calliope's sexy aunt' and 'the family black-sheep'. Her fascination only died when she came on a disturbing couple of paragraphs that suggested that her family had shut the door on her because she was a promiscuous wild-child.

Aristandros strode in, clad today in a dark pinstripe suit of faultless tailoring that made the most of his tall, well-built body. He was said to electrify a room when he walked into it, and Ella was certainly not immune to that effect. She tensed against the heaped-up pillows, sapphire-blue eyes very wide in the heart-shaped delicacy of her face.

'I've been working for four hours. One glimpse of you,' Aristandros husked, strolling over to the side of the bed, neatly sidestepping the sprinkle of discarded toys that betrayed Callie's visit earlier that morning, 'And I want to get straight back into bed.'

Her body tingled, nerve-endings uncurling in anticipation, heart rate speeding up. It was just sex, and she regularly told herself that fact. But she still had to acclimatise to the magnetic draw of wanting to rip his clothes off every time she saw him.

With an impatient sound he scooped up the heap of newspapers on her lap. 'Haven't you learned yet? You don't *ever* read your own publicity. I pay my lawyers to read it for me,' he confided, discarding the tumbled, crackling newspaper sheets in an untidy heap on the carpet. 'I did appreciate the Dr Dazzler line, but not the wild-child tag. Someone's confused you with your sister Susie, and an official apology will be appearing this week.'

Her full lower lip had parted from the upper. 'Are you saying you've complained?'

Aristandros shrugged and removed his jacket, pitching it on to the ottoman by the wall and removing his shoes. Smouldering dark-golden eyes assailed her as he straightened to his full six-foot-three-inches of height. 'I'm still convinced that you've only ever been a wild-child with me.'

'Well, you'd be wrong.'

'You're all talk and no action,' Aristandros quipped with a razor-edged challenge in his gaze. 'In bed you don't know how to do anything until I do it first!'

Cheeks as red as ripe strawberries, Ella slung him a

furious look. 'I suppose you think that that kind of crack is funny?'

'No, I find it highly entertaining that, while most women prefer to minimise the number of their past lovers, you want to claim more,' he drawled, smooth as silk.

'Why on earth are you getting undressed?' Ella demanded abruptly, finally taking notice of that fact.

'And, in spite of that scarlet past, she still has a mind as pure as driven snow. Haven't I corrupted you in any way?' Aristandros mocked, skimming off his boxers in a manoeuvre that soon made it blatantly obvious why he had stripped off.

'Oh…' A darting little frisson of sexual heat travelling through her slender length, Ella sank back into the pillows in a manner that might almost have been labelled inviting as he joined her in the bed.

'Oh…' Aristandros teased, reclining back and drawing her to him with clear intent. As her slim fingers found the bold, jutting length of his arousal, he emitted a roughened groan of appreciation. 'Oh *yes*,' he growled hungrily. 'You beat the hell out of a coffee break, *khriso mou*.'

For a split second, that quip made Ella hesitate, but in truth she found his sexual spontaneity and raw potency as irresistible as she found him. His sensual mouth on hers was like a brand that burned to create a flame that was never quite doused. No matter how much he kissed her, enough was never enough. His tongue thrust between her lips and released a flood of excitement that lit a feverish trail of response through her entire body. He wrenched her nightdress out of his path and closed his lips on a swollen pink nipple.

Sweet sensation gripped her while his knowing mouth

travelled between one taut peak and the other, laving and teasing her sensitised flesh until she moaned. With the impatient stroke of his forefinger, he probed the slick, wet welcome at the heart of her before pulling her under him with an unashamed urgency that thrilled her. He plunged into her hard and fast, and her eager body rose to meet his. Excitement was as intense and searing as a fire inside her. He pleasured her with long, forceful strokes, pushing back her knees to gain even deeper penetration. She felt like she had hitched a ride to the stars, and the spellbinding pleasure devoured her. She heard herself cry out and buck under him as breathtaking heat and the waves of ecstasy roared through her. In the sheer power of that sensual conflagration, she was helpless and mindless in her response. He slammed into her one last time with an uninhibited shout of satisfaction.

For a timeless moment she lay under him, rejoicing in his weight, the pound of his heart and the rasp of his breath. At that instant she felt as she often did, overwhelmed by the level of mind-blowing pleasure. But not so overwhelmed by physical sensation that she didn't enjoy the brush of his mouth against her brow in a salutation, and the tightening of his powerful arms around her in what might almost have been a hug. He didn't do hugs, but she lived in hope. She loved what he did to her in bed, but she loved the closeness in the aftermath even more, and never, ever stirred a muscle to break their connection before he did.

It was a shock when Aristandros tensed, voiced an unmistakeable Greek curse and pulled back from her in a violent movement that spoke more of rejection than of anything else.

Hard eyes struck her questioning gaze in a near-physical blow. He struck the wooden headboard with a powerful fist, and made her flinch back from him in consternation.

'What?' she gasped in bewilderment.

'I forgot to use a condom,' Aristandros bit out rawly.

'Oh…dear,' was all Ella could think to comment in that unbearably tense moment. The date when she was to start taking the contraceptive pill had not yet arrived, and she had warned him that other precautions would be necessary for the first couple of weeks they were together. Until now he had followed that rule with scrupulous care and had left no margin for error.

Aristandros sprang out of bed like a hungry tiger leaping on prey and swung round to glare at her. 'Is that all you've got to say?' he demanded icily. 'I don't want a child.'

A chill ran through Ella, and she wondered why that statement should feel like a slap in the face when she was equally as keen to avoid the trauma of an unplanned conception. She was frantically working out dates inside her head, which was difficult, as recent changes in her routine appeared to have unsettled her once-regular menstrual cycle. 'I'm afraid it probably wasn't the best time to overlook the precautions,' she admitted ruefully. 'I could be at my most fertile right now.'

'I can't believe I forgot!' Aristandros grated as if she hadn't spoken. 'I'm never careless.'

'Either of us could be infertile,' Ella remarked. 'You'd be surprised how common it is.'

Aristandros gave her a look of outrage and compressed his handsome mouth, as though the suggestion that he might not be able to father a child was a gross insult to his masculinity.

Ella stayed where she was until he had showered and departed. She was in shock, but she also felt that she had just received a much-needed wake-up call. For the past ten days she had been with Aristandros almost round the clock. He got up before six every morning to work with his personal staff. At eight, he joined Ella and Callie for breakfast. If he hadn't yet reached the stage of being able to totally relax and play with the little girl, he was at least unbending from his rigidity around her, and developing the ability to talk to her and get to know her.

Life on the vast luxury yacht was excessively comfortable and easy. The crew attended to their every need, and very often even before Ella realised that something was required or even available. She was waited on hand and foot and encouraged to be a lady of leisure, with nothing more important to consider than her next visit to the well-equipped beauty salon and its staff on the deck below. It was a lifestyle that could never have come naturally to her, but it gave her the opportunity to spend a great deal of time with Callie. The bond between Ella and her biological child already ran deep and strong. While she would never have chosen to frolic in a swimming pool for her own benefit, she was happy to do so when the purpose was to teach Callie to swim, and the occasions when Aristandros had joined them had proved by far the most entertaining.

'Sailing home to Greece' as Ari had termed it, had been more of a leisurely cruise than a straightforward trip between A and B. *Hellenic Lady* had called in at several islands. Aristandros had taken her out clubbing on Crete, and out to dinner on Corfu. Afterwards they had walked through the narrow streets of the old town hand-in-hand. And who had reached for his hand? Ella clamped cool palms to her agonised face. Hand holding? She felt ill. Just then her mortification was so intense that she honestly wanted to slap herself hard. How could she have been so stupid as to initiate such a foolish gesture? Romance had nothing to do with their relationship.

She was his mistress—the woman currently meeting the demands of his high-voltage sex drive—not his girl-friend, his fiancée or his wife. And, just as he had wanted, she was always sexually available, and not because she was afraid to be in breach of that outrageous contract that she had signed! No, indeed; the nagging hunger of desire that tormented her had nothing to do with contractual obligations or pride. She couldn't keep her hands off him, in or out of bed. The need to touch, to connect, was like a fever, a terrible temptation she fought day and night. She was appalled by how attached she had already become to being with Aristandros.

Yet nothing could have more clearly delineated the gulf between them than his reaction to the possibility of her falling pregnant. Somehow he had made her feel like a one-night stand he had picked up, a stranger she barely knew, a female body in which he had no interest once he had sated his most pressing sexual need. If she con-ceived, he would view it as a disastrous development, and she could only hope that the situation didn't arise.

Fresh from the shower and with a towel wrapped round her, she was walking back into the state room when Aristandros entered. 'Did I mention that I'm staging a social gathering at my Athens home this afternoon? No?' he queried lazily, when she gave him a look of frank dismay. 'I have some business to tie up with fellow investors and you'll be acting as my hostess.'

'Thanks for the last-minute warning!' Ella gasped.

'At least you don't need to worry about booking time in the beauty salon,' Aristandros quipped.

They flew from the yacht direct to the property. His villa on the Greek mainland was set in an unspoilt area of countryside. Surrounded by olive groves and vineyards, it enjoyed superb views of the mountains. Ella was surprised by the rural setting, for when she had last known Aristandros he and his grandfather had been very firmly rooted in the vast Xenakis townhouse in Athens.

'Drakon still prefers life in the city, but I like to escape the skyscrapers and the traffic at the end of the day, and here I'm still less than half an hour from the airport,' Aristandros advanced. 'I spend a lot of time on the island now. I can work from home, and it's very private.'

'It's beautiful here as well,' Ella commented, wondering just how many different properties he owned round the world, and even if he knew himself without having to think about it.

'The pearls look good on you.'

In receipt of that remark, Ella brushed the magnificent necklace at her throat with uneasy fingertips. It was matched by the pearl-drop earrings she wore, and most probably worth a fortune. A slender diamond-studded designer watch also encircled her wrist. She had no idea how much her growing collection of jewellery was worth, since nothing as vulgar as price was ever mentioned when Aristandros insisted on buying her a gift. The previous week an imposingly correct jeweller had flown out to the yacht with a magnificent selection of world-class gems for Ari's private examination. He had decided on the pearls, which were reputed once to have belonged to an Indian maharajah. Ella had already decided that when she and Aristandros parted she would leave all such unsolicited presents behind her.

Presumably Aristandros was accustomed to rewarding the women in his bed with gifts of extraordinary generosity. But the glorious jewels made her feel more like a trophy piece of arm-candy than ever, and frighteningly deserving of the offensive label her mother had fired at her: *Whore*. Was that how other people saw her as well—a costly parasite earning a rich reward for pleasing her tycoon lover in bed? She cringed inwardly at the suspicion that she had sunk so low. Ironically, at a moment when she was dressed from head to toe in designer clothing, and sporting fabulous gems, her once-healthy self-esteem was at a very low ebb. She was very much afraid that on Ari's terms she was just an expensive accoutrement, like a flash car—and, just as he only drove the world's most expensive cars, he wouldn't dream of showing off a woman without the spectacular looks, clothing and jewellery that paraded his wealth.

Catering staff already had the food and drinks for the reception organised. The house was immaculate, very contemporary in design, and perfect for large-scale entertainment. A svelte figure in a knee-length plum silk cocktail dress and stiletto heels, Ella joined Aristandros on the outside terrace where drinks were being served just as the first guests arrived. It was not very long before her cheeks were hot with self-consciousness. While everyone was scrupulously polite, it was brutally obvious that she was the focus of a great deal of curiosity. She tormented herself with worries of what stories might already have appeared in the local press about her. Ironically, it was the arrival of Ari's courteous grandfather, Drakon, which caused her the greatest embarrassment.

'Ella,' the dignified older man murmured, stooping to kiss her cheeks in a kindly salute of polished Xenakis charm. 'Is it rude to admit that, while I am delighted to renew our acquaintance, I very much regret meeting you in these circumstances?'

Lean, strong face broodingly dark and taut, Aristandros answered for her. 'Yes, it is rude, and quite unnecessary, Drakon. What circumstances?'

The elderly Greek's shrewd eyes withstood the challenge of his grandson's grim appraisal. 'Don't pretend to be obtuse, Ari,' he advised drily.

Rigid with mortification, and keen to escape the fallout and any further discussion, Ella was quick to move away to intercept Callie, who was toddling across the room to greet her. Helplessly smiling as the little girl came full tilt into her arms, Ella hugged her. Callie, adorable in a little blue-cotton dress, was as pretty as a picture, and already noticeably more confident and talkative than she had been when Ella had first met her. Callie expressed a desire for the toy rabbit that she took almost everywhere with her, and Ella was taking her back to Kasma to ask where it was when she heard the raised voices sounding from a room off the hall.

Behaving as if there was nothing untoward occurring,

the young nurse lifted Callie and took her back upstairs to look for the rabbit.

'If Callie is Ella's as you say,' Drakon Xenakis was thundering in Greek, 'Give her to Ella and let them both go!'

'I'm not prepared to let either of them go,' Aristandros drawled as quietly as if he was in church, his audible calm a striking contrast to his grandfather's anger. 'I had a very comprehensive agreement drawn up that suits Ella and I very well—'

'A *legal* agreement? Is this what I raised you to do— to corrupt a young woman who only wants access to her own child? Is this what it takes to appeal to your jaded appetites now, Ari? If you had a single streak of decency left, you would marry her, for you've destroyed her reputation!'

'The days when women needed to be whiter than white are long gone, Drakon. Thankfully I live in a world with far more enlightened sexual mores,' Aristandros retorted bitingly. 'Whether you believe it or otherwise, Ella is happy with me—'

'She's worth more than any of the gold-digging sluts you specialise in, and you're treating her worse than all of them! The only thing I see in this scenario is revenge, Ari…and it's ugly and unworthy of you.'

Nausea stirring in her stomach, and her blood running cold in her veins, Ella stumbled away from the partly open door before she could be caught in the act of eavesdropping. Drakon's opinion hit her as hard as a physical blow, because Ari's grandfather knew him well, indeed far better than she did. She had been quick to discard the idea of Aristandros acting in revenge—too quick? Certainly she had much preferred to believe that the secret of her ongoing attraction was more her being a *femme fatale* whom he had never forgotten. But how likely was that interpretation? Was it not more likely that Aristandros was taking revenge for her rejection all those years ago? He had made her walk away from her career, her home and even her principles. He had made her enjoy her captivity in the gilded cage of his life. No; he hadn't *made* her do anything, she acknowledged, trying to be honest with herself—she had made the choices she'd had to make to be with Callie, the daughter of her heart, and to be fair he had kept his promises.

Even so, revenge struck her as the more apt explanation for Ari's continuing interest in her. Why else would a man who could have the most beautiful women in the world settle for an inexperienced and unsophisticated doctor who was ill at ease with a party lifestyle? He would not have sacrificed his own desires and preferences for Callie's benefit. In fact, most probably Callie had merely been used as a weapon to put pressure on her biological mother. Having acquired the child, he had also acquired the perfect means to make Ella dance to his chosen tune, and that was exactly what he had done.

In the shaken-up state she was now in, it was the wrong moment for Ella to set eyes on her family for the first time in seven years. Her stepfather, a heavily built man with thick, grey hair, was standing on the terrace with a drink in his hand. Her mother, a slight, fair-haired woman in a pink dress, was by his side. Behind them stood two tall, dark young men—her half-brothers, grown to adulthood without her knowledge. Ella paled when Theo Sardelos looked right through her, and her mother, her face full of painful discomfiture, turned her head quite deliberately to avoid seeing her only surviving daughter. Her twin half-siblings, disdaining such pretences, stared stonily back at her, their scowling attitude one of pure belligerence.

Ella was very angry that Aristandros had put her family on the guest list without telling her. Conscious that she was not the only person present capable of noting that her family was giving her the cold shoulder, she forced herself to address her stepfather with a perfunctory greeting before turning to her mother to say, 'Would you like to come and see Callie?'

'No, she would not,' Theo Sardelos growled, slinging his stepdaughter a look of profound distaste as he answered for his wife, a controlling habit of his that Ella remembered with repulsion. 'Your presence here makes that impossible.'

Her olive branch broken and discarded unceremoniously at her feet, Ella did not respond. She knew the older man well enough to appreciate that he would relish any opportunity to embarrass her in front of an audience. Although it took considerable courage, she kept on smiling and moved on, beckoning a waiter to ensure a clutch of late arrivals were served at the buffet. Kasma brought Callie back down, and the little girl, her stuffed rabbit now tucked securely under her arm, sped back to Ella's side to clutch at her skirt in a possessive hold.

It took real effort for Ella to continue to play hostess and chat and smile as though nothing was wrong. Every so often she bent down to touch her hand gently on Callie's head and remind herself of what she had gained, and why she had forged her devil's bargain. Her thoughts were tumultuous. Aristandros had only told the truth to his grandfather: she *was* happy with him. Did that mean that at heart she was a slut? Sharing Ari's bed and being with him was more of a pleasure than a punishment. It shook her to admit that to herself. He had held her to ransom over an innocent child's head, and yet whenever he wanted her she was still his for the asking. What did that say about her? Shame and confusion engulfed her in a hot, creeping tide of remorse.

Lily had texted her only that day: *are you his Dr Dazzler by accident or design?*

Ella still didn't know how to answer that question. While the original design had been Ari's, it now sometimes seemed to her as though she had simply surrendered, and had used Callie as her excuse for doing so. When Aristandros touched her, she went up in flames. What had started out purporting to be a sacrifice had become a delight. If she was a victim, of revenge she was a willing victim and that reality made her cringe.

Lean, breathtakingly handsome face cool as icewater, his carriage as always superb, Aristandros strode towards her. Nothing in his expression revealed any sign of annoyance over his recent dispute with his grandfather. Her heart lurched behind her breastbone, her mouth running dry as he rested a hand at the base of her spine and whispered, 'Why aren't you with your family?'

CHAPTER EIGHT

ELLA shot him a darkling glance of disbelief. 'Why on earth did you invite my family when you knew there was a rift between us all?' she flung at him, half under her breath, furious that he had set her up for such a confrontation even after she had told him that her family was at odds with her and had been for years.

'I thought the invitation would help…I even thought you might be pleased to see them!' Aristandros responded, his strong face taut

'It was a serious mistake. You shouldn't have interfered. My family don't want to be around me when I'm with you,' Ella revealed in a bitter surge of confidence. 'In fact, Theo says they can't have anything to do with Callie while I'm here.'

Aristandros rested his stunned gaze on her, and swore below his breath. 'That's outrageous, *khriso mou*. He cannot insult you below my roof. Anyone who does so is an unwelcome guest.'

'There's not much you can do about it. He's a very stubborn man. Just ignore it, as I am, and hopefully in time he'll get over his pique. You shouldn't have asked them here.' Ella's teeth worried anxiously at her full lower lip as she absorbed the stormy flare of gold immediately lightening Ari's spectacular eyes. Assurances that he should *not have* done something went down like a brick with a guy who had based his entire life on doing what he wanted to do on every occasion. Callie vented a cross little sob and tugged at Ella's dress, while resting heavily up against her legs as tiredness took her over.

'Sardelos has upset you,' Aristandros growled. 'I will not tolerate that.'

'Stay out of this, it's not your business,' Ella hissed in a frantic undertone as she bent to comfort Callie, and lifted the child up into her arms. 'If you interfere any more it'll just cause endless trouble and resentment. I'm going to put Callie down for a nap. Promise me that you'll mind your own business.'

Aristandros dealt her a sardonic look of disbelief. 'You *are* my business. If they insult you, they insult me, for it is my wish that you be here and I will not tolerate any show of disrespect.'

Anchoring the little girl on her hip, and keeping her there with one straining arm—for Callie was no lightweight—Ella rested what she hoped was a soothing hand on his chest. 'Nobody is being disrespectful of you,' she hastened to assert in an effort to pour oil on troubled waters. 'Please don't get involved…*please*. Don't play with fire.'

With that final, urgent plea for forebearance, Ella headed off with Callie. Kasma offered to carry the little girl upstairs, but Ella demurred; in the mood she was in, the feel of Callie's clinging arms was comforting. The very last thing she needed was for Aristandros to wade in to an already delicate situation. She was all too pain-fully aware that her mother invariably suffered when Theo lost his temper

When she glanced down from the landing, she saw the male guests were gathering in the hall, and then moving on into Ari's office-suite, where a conference room would house the investors' meeting he had men-tioned. The sight of what had to be an excellent diver-sion for unreliable masculine tempers and egos filled her with a giant sense of relief. When business was at stake, Aristandros would surely not waste his energy thinking about anything else.

'Shoos,' Callie sounded importantly as Ella removed her sandals. 'Socks.'

'Very good,' Ella applauded, turning up Callie's earnest little face to drop a kiss on it.

'My goodness, she's talking now…'

Ella almost jumped out of her skin, and twisted her head round to focus on the older woman in the doorway. 'Mum?'

'Theo's gone into the meeting, and I asked a maid to bring me up,' Jane Sardelos explained in a harried under-tone. 'He would be furious if he knew I was here with you.'

'He gets furious far too easily. Why won't you leave him?' Ella asked in a pained, heartfelt undertone that betrayed her incomprehension on that score.

'He's my husband and he loves me. He's been a good father and provider. You don't understand,' the older woman proclaimed, just as she had throughout Ella's teenaged years. 'Let me see my grandchild… She's the very image of you, Ella.'

Ella noticed that the little girl showed no sign of recognising her grandmother. 'You haven't seen much of her, have you?'

'Susie was very difficult after the birth,' Jane murmured sadly as she stared down with softening eyes at the sleepy little girl and sat down beside the cot. 'She didn't want my advice, or anyone else's, and it was obvious that her marriage was breaking down and she didn't care. I saw Calliope a few times when she was very young, but Susie really didn't want to be bothered with visitors, and she was quite unpleasant on several occasions.'

'I think that Susie very probably had post-natal depression,' Ella contended gently.

'She wouldn't see a doctor, though.' Jane Sardelos shook her head heavily. 'I did what I could, but your sister was always very wilful and I'm afraid she paid the price for it. But I don't want you to pay a price as well.'

'Let's not talk about me,' Ella cut in hurriedly.

'Half the world is talking about you since you moved in with Ari Xenakis. He might want you today, Ella, but there are no guarantees for the next day, or the one after that. I shouldn't have called you what I did, but I was very upset when I found out that you were living with him.'

'I can't discuss Aristandros with you. I'm an adult and I've made my choice. I don't expect you to agree with it, but there's no point arguing about it, because it won't change anything. Mum, it's seven years since I even saw you,' Ella reminded the older woman painfully. 'Let's not waste this moment.'

'A moment is really all we have,' the older woman acknowledged tautly, scrambling up to wrap her arms round her taller daughter in a sudden jerky movement that betrayed the precarious state of her nerves. 'I've missed you so much, particularly after Susie passed away. But Theo is outraged by this situation. He says that because of your very public affair he's lost face.'

Ella hugged her mother back with warm affection. 'For goodness' sake, he always exaggerates—he is only my stepfather.'

'You've embarrassed the whole family,' another voice delivered in condemnation from the doorway.

Ella focused on her half-brother, Dmitri, as her mother backed away from her. 'Stop making excuses for your father,' Ella urged. 'He found fault with everything I ever did because I stood up to him. He doesn't like me and he never will.'

'Mum…in a few minutes Dad will be looking for you. You need to come back downstairs.' Having issued that warning, Dmitri turned away from Ella, who was livid with him for behaving like a pompous prat.

'Do you still live at home?' she asked her brother. Watching her mother turn pale with fear as she'd registered the risk of her husband discovering that she had defied his dictates took Ella back to all the years that she did not want to recall. Years blighted by sudden violence and discord, and Jane's increasingly pathetic attempts to make their warped family life seem normal.

'Not for years. Stavros and I have an apartment.'

'So, I can't ask you to look after Mum tonight,' Ella remarked stiffly.

Immediately grasping her meaning, Dmitri reddened, said nothing and concentrated on hurrying the older woman out of the room. He was as desperate to avoid conflict with his father as Ella had once been. She would

never forget the tension of living in the Sardelos household, where everyone had worked hard in speech and
action to avoid doing anything that might annoy Theo.
While the initial conflict in the marriage had arisen over
her stepfather's infidelity, he had soon found plenty of
other issues to set his temper off.

'I'll try to phone you.' Jane flung the promise over a
thin shoulder.

'Any time, and for any reason. I'll always be here for
you.' Ella returned that assurance with a slight wobble in
her strained voice. Until she had seen her mother again,
she had not allowed herself to acknowledge how much
she had missed the older woman's presence in her life.

Ella settled Callie for her nap, and left the nursery to
return to the female guests milling round the terrace and
the spacious drawing-room. She discovered that she
was very much the centre of attention, and was reminded of how curious people always were about
Aristandros—his lifestyle, his possessions, his women,
his family and background, all of which had supplied
years of gossip fodder for newspaper and magazine
articles. Tactfully sidestepping the more intrusive questions, she moved from one knot of women to the next.

The men filtered back in little groups to their
partners, and the guests began to go home. Drakon
Xenakis made a point of bidding Ella goodbye before
his departure. She was filled with consternation, however, when she saw her stepfather halt on the threshold
of the room and simply jerk his head in her mother's
direction in a peremptory signal that he wanted to leave.
Even at a glance she could tell that the older man was
incensed with anger, the colour high on his fleshy face,

his mouth compressed into an aggressive whitened line. As she watched her stepfather, her brothers and her mother trooped out without a further word to anyone.

Ella tracked Aristandros down to the office that connected with the conference room.

'What the heck did you say to my stepfather?' she demanded curtly.

His personal assistants froze in incredulity, and she flushed, wishing she had exercised greater self-control, and waited until she could speak to him alone.

Face impassive, Aristandros lounged back against the edge of the desk behind him and viewed her with hard, dark eyes. 'Don't address me in that tone,' he told her with a chilling bite.

Ella was mortified when only then did he dismiss his staff with a meaningful shift of one authoritative hand. 'I'm sorry,' she muttered. 'I should have waited a moment.'

'All that I ask is that you remember your manners,' Aristandros responded grimly.

'I was concerned—I saw Theo stomping out in a complete rage. What happened?' she pressed, anxiously pacing the carpet in front of him.

'I informed Sardelos and your brothers that they are not welcome here if they cannot treat you with respect.'

Ella shot him an appalled look. 'I don't need you to fight my battles for me!'

'I invited them, and this is my house. Their behaviour was unacceptable. What I say goes, *khriso mou*.' Aristandros spelt out that reminder without a second of hesitation

'I've never seen my stepfather so angry, and no wonder! You humiliated him in front of his sons, and he'll blame me for that as well!' Ella lamented. 'I could kill you for interfering in something that has nothing to do with you.'

'I defended you and you're behaving as if *I* did something wrong?' Aristandros growled, his eyes smouldering dark gold with angry disbelief. 'You've let your stepfather bully you for so long that you can't see the wood for the trees. He needs to be shown his boundaries by someone he can't influence or control.'

Ella spun away from Aristandros, her thoughts heavily preoccupied with the likely fallout from the comeuppance which Theo had been given. Her stepfather set great store on his association with the Xenakis family; the sudden loss of that favourable social standing would not only humble him but also harm his business prospects. She wanted to yell and shout at Aristandros for acting with a heavy hand, but knew he had no comprehension of the likelihood that her mother would ultimately pay for her husband's sins.

'You interfered by inviting them here when you knew there was a serious rift between us,' she accused tautly. 'For goodness' sake, my mother phoned me in Paris to tell me that they thought I was acting like a whore with you!'

Aristandros went rigid. 'A *whore*?'

'Nobody suffers from the illusion that *I'm* the one paying for the designer dresses and the jewellery!' Ella slashed back bitterly. 'How do you expect people to view me?'

His brilliant gaze semi-screened by his lush, black lashes, Aristandros stared broodingly back at her, his eloquent mouth clenching hard. 'It's not a question I paused to consider—'

Ella raised a dubious brow. 'You didn't? Well, my goodness, you considered everything else that related to image. Why else was I repackaged as a dress-up doll?'

But Aristandros wasn't listening. He was frowning darkly. 'So that's why you walked out on me in Paris…'

Ella tossed her head, her pale hair fanning back across a flushed cheekbone and brushed away by an impatient hand. 'That phone call may have made me a little touchier than I should have been.'

He treated her to an austere appraisal. 'But once again it underlines how little you listen to what I tell you, *khriso mou*.'

The intimidating tension in the atmosphere was ringing alarm-bells in Ella's head. Aware of his renewed anger, but at a loss as to its cause, she blinked in bemusement. 'I'm not sure I know what you're getting at.'

'That you should have told me about that phone call that distressed you,' Aristandros grated impatiently. 'And don't you *dare* tell me that it was none of my business, because your behaviour that night spoke for you! I don't like the way you keep secrets from me. It's dishonest.'

Ella sucked in a startled breath at that hard-hitting denunciation. She could not credit what he was saying to her. 'You have some nerve to say that to me!' she slung back. 'Maybe there's a lot about you I don't like: a guy who uses lawyers to blackmail me into an indefensible agreement to let him do whatever he likes, while I do *only* as he likes. Is that what you call having a relationship? No wonder none of them last longer than five minutes! On what basis do you think I would give you my trust?'

'Stop there before this gets blown out of all proportion,' Aristandros advised harshly.

But Ella was trembling with pent-up emotion, and she could no more have held back what she was feeling inside than she could have contained a tornado. Her blue eyes were as bright a blue as the heart of a flame. 'Do you think I could trust a man who once told me he loved me and wanted to marry me, but who dumped me less than an hour later? And why—because I couldn't match the perfect blueprint of a wife that you had in your head? Because I had the audacity to want something more than love and your money to focus on? Would you have given up business and the art of making money to marry me?'

Aristandros had lost colour below his bronzed skin, and it lent a curious ashen quality to his usual healthy glow. He stared steadily back at her, however, predictably not yielding an inch of ground. 'We're not having this conversation,' he told her.

'I'm not asking for permission, and I'm not having a conversation. You may not have noticed yet but I'm *shouting* at you!' Ella yelled at him at full tilt, inflamed by his stony resistance to her verbal attack and his refusal to respond.

'*Stamates*…that is enough,' Aristandros bit out icily.

'I hate you…even your grandfather thinks you're treating me badly… Yes—not content with having lousy manners, I listen outside doors as well!' Ella threw wildly at him, tears burning her eyes, and rage swelling like a giant balloon inside her to restrict her breathing. 'I'm definitely not the perfect woman you think is your due. You'd better pray that I'm not fertile!'

And with that final parting shot, which was as low as she could think to sink, Ella fled out past the clutch of his staff in the hall who were trying to act like everything was normal and avoid looking at her. She took the stairs two at a time, with a huge sob locked halfway up her throat, and raced into the master bedroom—her fourth since she had moved in with him.

Ella very rarely cried. A sad film or a book could make the moisture well up, but it took a great deal to make her cry. Now she flung herself across the bed and sobbed her heart out. She was worried about her mother having to go home alone with an enraged and violent man who liked to use her as a punch bag. But, most of all, she was distraught over the row she had just had with Aristandros. It had started out a small argument and just grown and grown until it had torn apart the fragile fabric of the peace they had established, and destroyed the bonds they had somehow contrived to build. Now there could be no hiding from ugly but revealing truths, such as his fear that she might conceive a child he didn't want.

Why was she getting upset over being at odds with him? At least she had spoken her mind on the trust issue. She had trusted him once seven years back and look where that had got her—dumped, heartbroken and rejected by her family. Aristandros, however, had picked himself up in time-honoured Xenakis style from the debacle of the engagement that had only lasted five minutes with a widely reported cruise round the Mediterranean, where he had stopped off at various ports to booze and carouse non-stop with promiscuous women. Ella struck the mattress with a clenched fist. She was still so angry she wanted to scream. She hated him; she truly *hated* him!

But it was almost time for Callie to have her evening

meal, and Ella cherished her bedtime routine with the toddler. She hauled herself off the bed and groaned out loud when she saw her swollen eyes and ruined make-up. No longer having access to the beautician's tools, and in possession of very few cosmetics of her own, Ella did her best to conceal the ravages of her uncontrolled crying-jag.

Callie was a delight and a consolation that evening. Ella played with her in her bath, dried her little wriggling body and cuddled the little girl while she read her a story.

Callie was happily making quacking sounds when Aristandros appeared on the nursery threshold. 'I fancy eating out tonight,' he announced.

'I don't care if I never eat again,' Ella lied, for in truth she was starving, but could not have borne letting him get away with pretending that nothing had happened—even if she did suspect that that might be a wiser approach than running the risk of a post mortem about the row.

Callie slid off her knee and padded barefoot over to him, holding her arms up and demanding to be lifted. Possibly relieved that someone appeared to appreciate his presence, Aristandros crouched down and swept her up into his arms as if he'd been doing it for years. But in fact he had never done it before, and Ella watched slyly from beneath her lashes as Callie explored his hair, smothered him in wet kisses and yanked at his tie before settling down happily, trying to steal one of his shiny gold cuff-links.

'Quack,' Callie told him importantly, and then she stuck out a foot. 'Socks,' she added.

'You're not wearing any,' Aristandros pointed out.

Callie pouted. 'Shoos.'

'You're not wearing shoes either.'

'She's trying to dazzle you with her new words, not have a conversation,' Ella explained.

'It's more appealing than conversation,' Aristandros remarked, shrewd dark eyes skimming from Callie's smiling little face to Ella's frozen expression. 'You're sulking again.'

'I'm not sulking,' Ella pronounced through gritted teeth. 'I'm just can't think of anything to say to you.'

'Is there a difference?' Aristandros strolled across the room to lower Callie gently back down on to Ella's lap. As their eyes connected in an unexpected encounter, she was shockingly aware of the raw charge of his masculinity, and her mouth ran dry.

'I'm going out,' he said casually.

Ella almost called him back to say that she would go out after all. Watching him go out alone had no appeal whatsoever. Her contentment at her relaxing session with Callie ebbed fast. No woman in their right mind would encourage Aristandros to go out by himself—but no woman with any pride would accompany him after the day that had just passed and the words that had been exchanged, Ella reasoned with spirit. When Callie was safely asleep she went downstairs and ate a light meal without appetite, while she watched the clock and wondered how long he would stay out and who he was with. Athens was a lively, cosmopolitan city with many clubs.

Having decided on an early night, she went for a bath, then phoned Lily and finally told her friend everything she had previously withheld.

'He's a total bastard!' Lily hissed in disgust.

Ella winced, finding that opinion not as much to her taste as she might have hoped. 'Occasionally he's...very challenging.'

'I don't believe what I'm hearing. You're making excuses for him?'

'That wasn't an excuse,' Ella protested uncomfortably.

'Ella...in all the years of our friendship I have never understood your essential indifference to men. Now, finally, I do. You're insanely in love with Ari Xenakis—and I do mean *insane*, because by the sound of it he's already running rings round you!'

'Of course I'm not in love with him,' Ella retorted crisply. 'We have absolutely nothing in common. He's cold, selfish and arrogant, and I could never care about a man like that!'

'On the other hand,' Aristandros added lazily, striding into the bedroom without warning and startling her into dropping the phone, 'I'm very rich, very clever and very good in bed—a combination of traits which seems to keep you very well entertained, *khriso mou*.'

Ella fumbled clumsily for the phone again.

'It's okay...I heard,' Lily admitted. 'I think you've just met your match, Ella.'

Ella replaced the phone and stared at Aristandros. Her nipples stirred and peaked below her nightdress, becoming uncomfortably sensitive. His scrutiny burned like molten gold over her upturned face, and pink colour warmed her cheeks while her tummy performed a wicked little somersault of response. The atmosphere sizzled. She closed her eyes tight and snuggled down beneath the sheet, awesomely conscious of his presence, and tensing to the rigidity of an iron bar when the mattress gave under his weight

'*Se thelo*…I want you,' Aristandros breathed thickly as he eased her back into his arms.

'I thought you'd be out half the night,' she framed flatly, staying stiff and unresponsive against the hard, muscular heat of him.

'Not when you're in my bed waiting for me, *moli mou*.'

'I wasn't waiting for you!' she yelped.

Brushing back her tumbled silvery-blonde hair, he pressed his sensual mouth to the slender column of her neck, and she quivered beneath the erotic brush of his lips across her skin. 'Of course you were. Do you think I don't know when a woman wants me?'

'Quack,' Ella pronounced flatly.

Aristandros vented a husky laugh above her head. 'Meaning?'

'That normal dialogue is a waste of breath with a guy as vain and arrogant as you are.'

Aristandros extracted her from her nightdress without receiving or even appearing to need the smallest assistance from her. He proved that he was more than capable of rolling with the punches of that negative character-assessment. He nibbled at the tender skin below her ear, while his hands roved from the urgent jut of her swollen nipples to the slick, wet flesh between her thighs. She clenched her teeth and gasped, striving to resist temptation until he teased the tiny nub of arousal below her feminine mound, and suddenly resistance was more than she could bear. She twisted round in a violent movement and found his tormenting mouth for herself, burning for him and burning with shame simultaneously. He held her to him with strong hands and plundered her parted lips until she was breathless with desire. Then he lifted her over him and pushed up into her slick, tight depths with a long, guttural groan of pleasure.

'As long as you know that I still hate you,' Ella mumbled shakily, struggling not to lose herself entirely in the pleasure he had unleashed.

'I love the way you hate me,' Aristandros husked, long, brown fingers on her hips controlling her rhythm, and then rising to cup her swaying breasts and roll the sensitive crests.

She was dizzy with excitement and beyond thought. The waves of pulsating pleasure began low in her pelvis and slowly spread out in ever-increasing circles in a white-hot surge of shattering pleasure. She cried out, and her head fell back on her shoulders as the wild convulsions of ecstasy engulfed her.

Aristandros cradled her limp body and rolled over to a cooler spot in the big bed. 'Tomorrow we'll be on Lykos, and I don't think I'll let you out of bed for a week. You make me insatiable, *khriso mou*.'

Her brain kicked back into gear and she flinched, loathing herself for surrendering to the passion. 'I meant everything I said,' she told him doggedly.

'What a temper you have,' Aristandros mused lazily, his unconcern on that score palpable.

Her body still throbbing from the primal urgency of his possession, Ella pulled free of him and shifted over to the far side of the bed.

'No,' Aristandros said succinctly, and he reached for her with hands that brooked no argument and hauled her bodily back into contact with his long, powerful body. 'What you sow, you must reap, and I'm not finished yet.'

'I am!' But, as she spoke, the familiar signature tune she used on her mobile phone broke out in the tense silence.

'Ignore it,' Aristandros instructed. 'It's after midnight.'

Ella, by comparison, was accustomed to reacting with urgency to calls during the night, and she broke from his loosened hold and snatched up the flashing mobile-phone on the bedside table to answer it. An instant later, she threw her legs off the side of the bed and stood up to switch on the lamp. Although she couldn't yet understand what her mother was saying, she realised that the older woman was crying and that something was badly wrong.

'Calm down; I can't follow what you're saying. What happened? Did he hit you?'

Ella felt Aristandros pull himself up behind her. 'Are you still in the house?' she prompted her parent. 'Where is Theo? Look, whatever you do, don't go back in there,' Ella warned the weeping older woman. 'Stay where you are and I'll come and get you. No, of course it isn't a problem. Don't be silly, Mum. All I care about is you.' Putting her phone down, she turned to Aristandros. 'I need a car.'

Aristandros was already talking into the house phone and getting out of bed. He broke off to demand, 'Did Sardelos attack your mother? What happened?'

'What always happens,' Ella responded wearily. 'He has a few drinks, blames her for everything wrong in his life and hits her. He's in bed. She's in the park across the street. Why are you getting dressed?'

'I'm coming with you.'

Ella was already pulling on a pair of trousers. 'That's not a good idea.'

His handsome features were grim. 'I'm not leaving you to handle this alone. Your stepfather left my house in a rage this evening, and I was to blame for that.'

'You're not to blame for anything. Theo is the baddie here. I warn you: Mum won't report him to the police. I've tried a dozen times to persuade her to have him charged, but she won't, so he gets away with it every time. She's like an addict,' Ella muttered heavily. 'She won't give him up.'

'Are you planning to call your brothers?'

'I'll do what Mum wants me to do. I notice she phoned me rather than either of her sons.'

Twenty minutes later, Ella was approaching the park bench where her mother was huddled like an old discarded rug, her shoulders hunched, her head bent, so that even in the street light her face couldn't be seen. When Ella got her first proper look at her, she had to bite back an exclamation. Her face swollen and puffy with one eye almost sealed shut, Jane Sardelos was almost unrecognisable. Her lip was cut and distended, and she was cradling one arm as though it was hurting her.

'What's up with your arm?' Ella asked.

'Let's get her into the car first,' Aristandros urged.

'You brought him with you?' the older woman gasped in horror.

'I couldn't shake him off.' Ella helped her mother stand up and guided her towards the waiting limo. Once they were safe in the passenger seat, she bent to examine the arm and realised that the older woman's wrist was badly broken. 'We'll have to go to the hospital.'

'No hospital…I'll go to a hotel or something.'

'You don't have a choice,' Ella broke in. 'I think your wrist needs surgery, and the sooner it's done the better. Do you want me to call the boys?'

Jane shook her head in an urgent negative. 'No point in upsetting them as well.'

Aristandros raised a brow but made no comment. During the drive to the hospital and then their subsequent arrival, after he had called in advance, she was surprised by how gentle he was with her battered mother, who had never been one of his biggest fans. She was wryly amused when his natural charm began to draw the older woman out of her shell.

It was a very long night. After the x-rays had been carried out, Jane was given a thorough examination, and Ella was appalled by the bruising she saw on her parent's thin body. It was obvious to her that, if anything, her stepfather's attacks had become even more violent over the years. Surgery was immediately scheduled for her wrist. The police arrived beforehand, and Ella braced herself for her mother's usual evasive efforts to shield her husband from arrest and prosecution. Aristandros asked if he could speak to Jane privately for a moment and Ella stepped outside the room, curious as to his motive, but so sleepy that she was grateful for the chance to move around and wake up a bit.

She was shocked when she realised on her return that her mother was finally willing to give a true statement of events and press charges against Theo. She also seemed stronger, steadier and less afraid than she had been. While she was in the operating theatre, Aristandros made a series of phone calls.

'What did you talk about with Mum?' Ella asked.

'She wants a fresh start, and I pointed out that she can't have it without having Sardelos charged with assault, because only that will make him leave her alone. I also pointed out that she could well die during one of his assaults. I asked her to accompany us to Lykos to recuperate, but she wants to stay with your brothers until she's feeling better. I called them. They should be here soon.'

Ella was disappointed that Jane wouldn't be coming to the island, but she knew that her mother would very much enjoy fussing over her adult sons for a few weeks. She was amazed that Aristandros had triumphed where she had so often tried and failed. Her stepfather was finally going to be taken to court, and that was a source of tremendous relief to Ella. But perhaps it wasn't so strange, she conceded. Jane was always more easily impressed by a strong man than she was by a strong woman, and Ari's intervention and advice had been warmly appreciated and respected.

They remained at the hospital until Jane emerged from the operating theatre and had regained consciousness in the recovery room. The surgery had been long and complicated but successful. Ella fell asleep in the limousine, and wakened only when Aristandros settled her down on the bed.

'You were really great tonight with Mum,' she mumbled drowsily. 'I wasn't expecting that.'

'I'm not always the bastard you like to think I am,' Aristandros retorted with level cool.

Her heavy limbs sinking into the comfortable mattress,

Ella focused wryly on his lean, compellingly handsome face. 'I'm not stupid,' she told him. 'Leopards don't change their spots.'

CHAPTER NINE

THE island of Lykos had undergone some changes since Ella's last visit seven years earlier. Aristandros had made the harbour much bigger and deeper to accommodate his yachts. The fishing boats looked like colourful children's toys beside *Hellenic Lady*. The island's little town, composed of lime-washed white houses adorned with traditional blue paintwork, stretched up the hill in neat tiers behind the harbour. The wedding-cake church with its ornamental bell tower sat in the shade of the plane trees edging the main square, and a windmill, long defunct but nonetheless charming, punctuated the winding road that led down to the far end of the island and the Xenakis house. Beyond the town stretched lush green hills studded with cypresses and olive groves and rather more buildings than she recalled.

'The last time we were here you told me that you wanted to get married in a church exactly like that,' Aristandros murmured.

'Did I…really?' Standing by the rail as the yacht docked, Ella was still suffering from the loss of the previous night's sleep. That reminder almost made her choke on the coffee she was drinking to wake herself up, and she secretly cringed over the knowledge that she could ever have been that gauche. 'I don't remember that.'

'I liked the fact that you didn't watch your every word around me. My parents got married here in the church of Ayia Sophia. My mother thought it was cute as well.'

'Lykos originally belonged to her family, didn't it?'

'Yes. She was an only child and a great disappointment to a shipping family, who longed for a son.'

'I just remember the portrait of her in the house. She was absolutely gorgeous.'

'She still holds the trophy for being the vainest woman I ever knew,' Aristandros remarked with a cynical shake of his proud dark head. 'In many ways she was lucky to die young. She could never have handled growing old.'

Ella thought it was sad that he could be so detached from the memory of his mother, a habit he had probably acquired for self-protection when he was a boy, cursed by not one but two wildly irresponsible parents who had refused to grow up and behave like adults. Too alike to stand each other for long, the warring pair had divorced by the time he was five years old.

Although Doria Xenakis had grown up with great beauty and wealth, both attributes had only been a means to an end for a young woman obsessed by her dream of becoming a famous actress. While his mother had chased endless drama-classes and roles, and thrown constant parties to entertain influential celebrities, Aristandros had been seriously neglected. He had twice been removed from her home by social workers for his own safety. Doria had finally died of a drug overdose at the age of thirty, and was only remembered in the film world for having starred in some of the worst movies ever made. Ari's father, Achilles Xenakis, an inveterate gambler, womaniser and drunk, had worked his way through multiple partners and repeated visits to rehabilitation centres after an unending succession of financial and sexual scandals. Achilles had died when he crashed his speedboat. Orphaned, Aristandros had moved in with Drakon at the age of fourteen.

Ella, Callie and Aristandros climbed into one of the cars waiting by the harbour while their luggage was stowed in another. Ella gazed out at the turquoise-blue sea washing the inviting white strand that circled more than half the island and, appreciating its emptiness, said, 'Are you still trying to keep the tourists out?'

'Why would I want to share paradise?'

'It would be the easiest way of revitalising the economy and persuading the younger people to stay on. A small, exclusive development near the town wouldn't interfere with your privacy.'

'Remind me to keep you well away from the town council. They'd elect you immediately,' Aristandros asserted. 'In recent years, I've brought in several businesses to provide employment, and the population is currently thriving—without the tourist trade and its attendant problems.'

Ella gave him a sunny smile. 'I'm sure you know what works best in your own personal little kingdom.'

'I do not regard the island as my kingdom,' Aristandros growled.

'I didn't mean to be controversial,' Ella declared unconvincingly.

Aristandros skated a long, reproving forefinger along one slender thigh clad in coffee-coloured linen trousers. 'Liar. You always liked getting under my skin, *moli mou.*'

'Constant agreement and admiration is bad for you. Too many people behave as if your every decision is an act of sheer brilliance.'

'It usually is,' Aristandros fielded. 'That's how I make so much money.'

Involuntarily, Ella grinned, for his self-assurance was immense and always bold as brass. She studied the big house perched like a land-locked ship on the cypress-studded hillside. The villa, designed by his late mother, overlooked a secluded cove where the clear waters reflected the sky.

'I have a project for you while you're here,' he said, greeting the staff assembled in the hall while Ella retrieved Callie from surging towards the stairs as fast as her little feet could carry her. 'Revamp the house and drag it out of the eighties. It always reminds me of a film set.'

The big screen was undoubtedly what had inspired his mother's opulent choice of décor, and the vast sunken living-area, marble floors and theatrical Greek columns. Ella was amazed that he had still not had the house renovated, and it made her wonder if he was more sentimental than he would ever be willing to admit. Doria's portrait still adorned one wall, along with many photographs of her taken with famous people.

Aristandros bore not the slightest resemblance to his blonde, brown-eyed mother. He did, however, look very like his handsome father. In terms of attractiveness, though, he easily outshone both his parents, Ella decided, shooting him a keen appraisal. While he had Achilles' looks, he had inherited his grandfather's sharp intelligence and business acumen. Daily exposure to Aristandros had simply made her more aware than ever that he was an extravagantly beautiful, intriguingly clever and challenging man. On paper he ticked all her boxes.

Turning pink as he intercepted her lingering scrutiny, Ella walked out hurriedly on to the sweeping terrace and wondered if Lily was right: was it possible that she had never got over loving Aristandros? Had she never moved on properly after that first disillusionment? The suspicion appalled her, for she liked to see herself as being sensible. The sort of woman who could continue to harbour a strong, secret preference for a notorious womaniser struck Ella as being silly, weak in resolution and certifiably insane.

'In three weeks' time we'll be attending a major charity performance at the opera in aid of the Xenakis Foundation. Dress formal,' Aristandros announced.

Ella suppressed a sigh. 'Where's it being held?'

'Athens.'

Ella saw Callie installed in the nursery, which the little girl clearly saw as home. Callie toddled over to a basket of toys and smiled as she dug out familiar favourites, her satisfaction at rediscovering them unhidden. Later, when Callie was in bed and Ella was dining out on the terrace with Aristandros, she breathed in deep. 'You know, I've barely been with you two weeks and this will be the sixth different bed I've slept in.'

Aristandros shifted a broad shoulder with nonchalant cool. 'Change is stimulating.'

'I know you don't want to hear this…'

Aristandros shifted a fluid brown hand in a silencing gesture. 'Then don't say it,' he advised drily.

'It's not fair to Callie. She needs a more settled home.'

'I don't normally trail her round the world with me as I have done recently,' Aristandros finally admitted. 'She's usually based here on the island.'

Guilt assailed Ella as she grasped the heart of the dilemma. 'She's travelling because I'm in the picture now and you know I want to be with her,' she guessed ruefully.

'While I want you to be with me. We're the perfect threesome,' he quipped. 'Be practical.'

Ella toyed with her delicious, light seafood starter, her appetite ebbing. *Be practical—remember the agreement you signed, remember who calls the shots around here, remember who says what goes as far as Callie's concerned.* But his lifestyle was unsustainable for a toddler, Ella reflected. More than anything Callie needed stability and routine to thrive, not to mention the same people around her.

Dark eyes reflective, Aristandros sipped his wine. 'I have a business trip next week. I'll leave you here.'

'Great.' Ella knew she was being thrown a consolation prize, but ironically she just as quickly found herself wondering whether his sudden willingness to leave her behind could relate to the fact that he was getting a little bored with her. Why not? she asked herself. Two weeks was a sizeable length of time for Aristandros to stay committed to one woman. And, if he was losing interest, how would she handle it?

Extinguishing that incendiary thought from her mind, for she saw no advantage in borrowing trouble in advance, she phoned her mother, who was still in hospital, after dinner. Jane was in reasonable spirits. Stavros and Dmitri were visiting her and had passed on the news that their father had been arrested and charged. Freed from the fear of her husband's violence, Jane had decided to go for counselling.

'Mum's dealing with this better than I thought she would,' Ella commented to Aristandros when he wandered out of the bathroom, only a towel linked round his lean hips and drops of water still sparkling on his hair-roughened chest. She would never have dreamt of adding that her mother thought she had misjudged him seven years earlier and had underestimated his potential for reliability. In her mother's eyes, Aristandros had suddenly become a knight in shining armour worthy of the highest praise.

'Hopefully it will give her a new lease of life. Sardelos had sucked all the energy out of her,' he pronounced grimly.

A slender figure in a shimmering emerald-green nightdress edged with lace, Ella shivered. 'I was only a child when they married, but I still remember how different she was before she met him—lively and outgoing. He turned her into a doormat.'

'Not something anyone could accuse you of.'

Her blood sang in her veins as she studied him. He made her feel like a teenager—a hopelessly infatuated teenager, who got a thrill every time he looked at her. 'Sometimes you make me very angry.'

A wicked grin slashed his handsome mouth, and her heart hammered as if he had pressed a switch. 'You make me hot in a very different way, *khriso mou*.'

For the first time Ella took the initiative, crossing the room to slide up against his hard, masculine body, revelling in every point of physical connection with an earthy streak she hadn't known she possessed until he'd brought it out in her. The very boldness of his arousal thrilled her. He parted her lips and let his tongue delve hungrily, deeply, and her bones seemed to melt beneath her skin while languorous heat and heaviness slowly uncoiled between her thighs. She detached the towel and looked up at him while she traced the impressive length of his erection.

'There's no hope for you in the wanton stakes,' Aristandros husked. 'You're still blushing.'

'Of course I'm going to blush if you're planning to offer a running commentary!'

'So, take my breath away, *moli mou*.'

And she did, kneeling down gracefully at his feet to deploy her slim hands and her full, sensual mouth to the task she had set herself. She used her knowledge of the male physique and her infinitely more intimate aware-ness of what he liked to pleasure him. Ella was always a high achiever at anything she set out to do. Ripples of helpless response began shuddering through his power-ful frame. He withstood her provocative attention for a very short time. His breathing audibly fractured, and then suddenly he was pulling her up and backing her down on the bed with scant ceremony.

'You excite the hell out of me!' he groaned, coming down on top of her and ravaging her luscious pink mouth until her senses swam.

He made love to her with mind-blowing power. Afterwards she lay shell-shocked with the intensity of the pleasure in his arms, her willowy body magically indolent and peaceful after her explosive release. He smoothed her hair gently back off her warm face. She kissed a smooth, muscular shoulder, catching the faint scent of cologne mingled with his own male scent, and drank in the smell of him like an addict. Right and wrong, she registered, no longer seemed so well-defined.

On some level she couldn't hold back what she was feeling any longer, and wasn't even sure that there was a point in such restraint while she lived with him and Callie. Sexually she found him irresistible, but his hold on her went much deeper than that. She was possessive of him and she cared about him as she had never yet cared for any other man. Yet he wasn't the young man she had fallen in love with any more. Those seven years apart had altered him. He was harder, more cynical and self-contained, and willing to go to any lengths to get what he wanted. Was it terribly wrong of her to feel special because he had gone to such extremes to get her back into his life again? And what was he doing to her once-firm moral compass?

In the early hours of the following morning she wakened and frowned at the familiar little cramping pains low in her stomach. A moment later she got out of bed and went into the bathroom to check out her suspicions. No, as she had thought, she wasn't pregnant, and it was time to start her contraceptive pill. The necessities taken care of, she returned to bed.

Aristandros was still fast asleep in a careless sprawl which took up more than his fair share of the bed, outsized though it was. With his jet-dark lashes almost long enough to hit his hard cheekbones, blue-black stubble outlining his angular jaw and sculpted mouth, and with his classic, aquiline profile relaxed, he looked gorgeous. Her insides chilled at the thought of how he might have reacted to an inconvenient pregnancy. He liked to control everything, and she couldn't have allowed him to exert control or influence in that field. She was grateful that the situation hadn't arisen.

'Hmm…' He shifted position and found her, a hand splaying across her stomach and then rising to cup a small, firm breast with a drowsy sound of masculine contentment. '*Ella*…'

'I'm not pregnant!' Ella just blurted it out, keen to get the news out, mortified by the idea that he was secretly dreading the possibility that she might have conceived.

Spiky black lashes lifted on startled dark-golden eyes. He was as instantly awake as if she had doused him with a bucket of cold water. 'Are you sure?'

'One hundred percent,' she declared.

His lean, strong face clenched. 'I would have taken care of you. You needn't have worried on that score.'

'We have enough problems without that particular one.'

'You still don't want children?'

'I didn't say that.'

'Just not children with me?' His expression sardonic, Aristandros released her and vaulted out of bed. 'I need a shower.'

Ella was bewildered by his behaviour. 'I assumed you would regard a pregnancy as a disaster and that you'd ask me to have a termination. You did tell me you didn't want a child.'

A bronzed vision of pagan masculinity, he surveyed her with brooding force from the bathroom doorway, and shrugged a broad shoulder. 'Then I thought about it and I reckoned I could live with it. Callie would probably enjoy having a playmate,' he murmured lazily.

'I wouldn't have suggested a termination. The main reason my father divorced my mother was that she tried to have me aborted—he stopped her on the way to the clinic. That kind of knowledge gives you a different take on an accidental pregnancy.'

Shocked by the content of that entire speech, Ella nodded slowly. 'I suppose it would.'

She tried to get her thoughts in order. Every time she thought she had Ari pigeon-holed, he confounded her expectations again. Think of him casually commenting that Callie would enjoy a playmate, admitting that, at the very least, he was uncomfortable with the idea of terminating a pregnancy that was merely inconvenient! *I reckoned I could live with it*—he could live with her having his baby. Well, she was still relieved that she wasn't about to face that challenge. He would have needed to be a good deal more enthusiastic and they would have had to have discussed the idea in advance before she could have allowed herself to regret the fact that she hadn't conceived.

Swallowing hard, she got back into bed. She had on several occasions in recent years gone through the experience of feeling broody, when the very sight of a baby or tiny clothes brought a lump to her throat and a powerful craving, but she would never have admitted anything so personal to him. Indeed her longing to see and hold her biological daughter had almost broken her heart for eighteen months. But, now fully aware of how incredibly lucky she was to have a loving healthy child like Callie in her life, she expected nothing more from Mother Nature.

Ella prowled round the modern building housing the doctor's surgery and emergency facilities which

Aristandros had funded on the outskirts of town. It was a rural doctor's dream, but apparently two doctors had already come and gone, bored with the lack of a social life on a small island and the inconvenience of having to step on a ferry to visit friends and family. Currently the position was vacant. Having checked out the patient numbers, Ella reckoned there was really only enough work for a part-time doctor, and she very much would have liked to put her name forward.

'We would be honoured to have you here,' the town mayor, Yannis Mitropoulos, assured her, having intercepted her and offered her a tour after she had been seen peering wistfully through a window.

'Unfortunately, I'm not looking for a job at present,' Ella advanced uncomfortably.

Had she been, she was convinced she would have been in harness within five minutes of accepting the job. Aristandros had devoted two days to showing her round the island, and had introduced her to many of the locals. But he had *not*, offered her an inspection of the unoccupied state-of-the-art medical building he had built, or admitted that Lykos lacked a doctor's services. Ella had only found out those facts for herself when she'd taken Callie into town. Whilst enjoying cold drinks at the taverna overlooking the picturesque harbour, she had found herself slowly and steadily being surrounded by hopeful people in search of off-the-cuff medical advice. Aristandros, however, appeared to have no conscience about keeping the only doctor on the island confined to home, hearth and bedroom.

In spite of that truth, over the past three weeks Ella had settled happily into life on Lykos. Aristandros had twice flown off on business trips without her, and she had been dismayed by the discovery that she missed him when he was out of reach. He was, however, surprisingly sexy and amazingly addictive during late-night phone conversations, she conceded with a covert smile.

She had come to terms with the fact that she loved him, and that she probably loved him a great deal more than she had seven years ago, which struck her as especially ironic when he had behaved so badly this time round. Back then she had expected perfection, a soulmate who shared her every thought and conviction and made no awkward demands of her. Now her expectations were rather more human-sized and, in any case, she knew that she and Aristandros were diametrically opposed by the simple fact that she was a modern female and he was very old-style macho male. Although she felt that Aristandros was being totally selfish and unreasonable in refusing to allow her to pursue her medical vocation, she was beginning to suspect that his being the centre of her world, the only other person she really had to think about besides Callie, was something he prized above everything else in their relationship. He was as possessive as she was, and seemingly unwilling to share her.

Ella had managed to adopt two homeless dogs since her arrival on Lykos. One, Whistler, a fluffy mongrel of indeterminate breed, had been injured by a fish hook and brought to her for attention for there was no vet on the island either. Ella had dealt with the little animal's lacerations and had offered to keep her while she healed. The second dog had arrived on the slender strength of the assurance that 'everybody knows the English are mad about dogs'. Bunny, inappropriately named by

Callie, was a boisterous Great Dane pup with paws the size of dinner plates, and he was accused of having sneaked off the ferry unattended. Both dogs were brilliant with Callie.

Aristandros had been taken aback by the sudden addition of two animals to the household, but had adapted wonderfully well after a lot of cool brow-raising over their antics, and had admitted that his mother had hated dogs and that he had never been allowed a pet. Ella thought his heart had been touched by Callie's enthusiasm for the dogs: the sight of the trio gambolling on the beach was quite something.

Of course Aristandros was learning to love Callie which was very entertaining to watch. For instance, he tried to teach Callie to say 'toes' and she continually came up with 'socks' or 'shoes'. She saw his pleasure when her daughter rushed to greet him and hug his knees. The child's innocent affection and playfulness drew him out of his cynical shell and made him patient and much less driven. When his mobile phone had been found in a vase of flowers, he'd insisted he had somehow dropped it in there, when everyone in the house knew that Callie was always trying to get her hands on his phone because the colours it flashed attracted her like a magnet.

It no longer mattered to Ella that Aristandros had fenced her in with an outrageous legal agreement. She had signed up for the long haul and was beginning to dare to hope that he might have as well. She was happier with him than she had ever dreamt she could be. The gift of a grand piano had been his most well-received present to date, and she was able to play her music every day on a superb instrument with wonderful tone, and she was already looking forward to teaching Callie. But the piano was only one of a number of fabulous presents with which he had surprised her. She had acquired designer handbags, perfume, sundry outfits and a fantastic sculpture of a sylph-like dancer that he had said reminded him of her. As she did not have endless legs and a large bosom quite out of proportion to the rest of her body, she had decided to be flattered by the unlikely comparison.

Aristandros was now accustomed to seeing her without make-up or a fancy hair-do, but dressed instead in casual beach-wear or jeans, and none of it had put a single dent in her apparent desirability. Her mother and her twin siblings had visited, and he had taken her brothers—who were not the world's most entertaining guys, out fishing and sailing without even being asked. She had been grateful, for her family now accepted their relationship, which made life a great deal smoother.

He had proved surprisingly understanding when she had been overjoyed after receiving a letter forwarded by Lily from Alister Marlow. As asked, Alister had notified the cleaner about the photo Ella had mislaid, and the small, faded snapshot of her late father had been found behind a piece of furniture. Ari had been sympathetic when he'd grasped that Ella had no memory of her father, who had died when she was only a baby. He, too, had been a doctor.

'Is that why you went in for medicine?' Aristandros had asked.

'No, I wanted to be a doctor from quite a young age, and as I got older it appealed more and more. I loved the idea of being able to fix people's bodies and solve their problems, but of course it's only occasionally that straightforward.'

But, when it came to the lack of commitment in relationships that Ella saw as Ari's most pressing problem, she convinced herself that she had the solution. If their sex life was good, Ari would surely have no reason to stray—but she despised herself for thinking that way and for being willing to accept those boundaries. Her pride told her she deserved more, but her brain told her that she already had as much as she could reasonably expect from Aristandros Xenakis in terms of attraction, attention and time. Even the newspapers were talking about what a quiet life he was leading of late.

In honour of the charity opera performance she was to attend that very evening, she had shopped for hours in Athens for a gorgeous dress and had promised to wear the sapphires with it. Aristandros had flown out the night before on a helicopter, and she was being picked up early evening. The beautician who worked on *Hellenic Lady* came to the house to do the honours, and Ella was admiring how well her hair looked when Ianthe, the housekeeper, came to her bedroom to tell her that Yannis Mitropoulos had phoned to ask if she would come and see his daughter who was pregnant and unwell.

Ella wasted no time in driving into the town to the surgery, with Ianthe in tow. Grigoria was a young first-time mother-to-be who was almost eight months' pregnant with twins. Her husband was in the army and away from home. Grigoria was very nearly hysterical, and clung so tightly to Ella that she had to prise herself free to examine her patient. What she learned was not good. Grigoria's blood pressure was sky high, and her hands and feet were swollen. Her condition was made more complex by the fact that she was a diabetic. Ella told Yannis that they needed the air ambulance, for she was convinced that his daughter was suffering from pre-eclampsia and needed urgent hospital treatment. It was a dangerous condition which would most likely only be cured by the delivery of the babies. She checked the records and rang the relevant hospital to forewarn them and get the advice of the gynaecologist on duty.

'You'll come with me?' Grigoria pleaded, clutching at Ella's arm frantically.

'I would be very grateful if you would,' Yannis added jerkily, tears in his eyes as he took her to one side and began to tell the very sad story of how his late wife had once gone on the same journey and, for possibly the same reason, and had died shortly after Grigoria's birth.

His daughter's state of mind was not helped by that inopportune recollection of her mother's demise. Ianthe ventured to remind Ella of the opera engagement, and the reminder cleared Ella's frown away; she was quick to work out how she could be in virtually two places at once, for both destinations were in the city. Determined to stay with Grigoria, Ella instructed the housekeeper to have her evening dress and jewellery delivered to Ari's house in Athens where she would be able to change for the evening, having left the hospital.

The flight in the air ambulance to Athens was fraught and tense; Grigoria was suffering increasing pain, and was seriously ill. It was a great relief to reach the hospital. Ella, preoccupied with her patient's condition, spared not a thought for her disrupted social arrangements until Grigoria's twins, two little girls, were safely delivered by Caesarean section. Her anxiety about Grigoria soothed by the knowledge that the young woman was receiving the best possible treatment, Ella only then registered that she had not even tried to contact Aristandros to tell him where she was. In a passion of dismay that she had been so thoughtless in relation to an engagement which he had made clear was an important event, she texted fervent humble apologies to him. She wasted no time trying to explain what had happened, but instead promised to join him by the time of the intermission.

More precious time was wasted while she found a taxi willing to take her out of the city. She contacted Ianthe to check that the dress had been delivered. Reassured on that score, Ella began worrying about how Aristandros would react to her appearance just before the end of the evening. Her heart sank. He hadn't responded to her text, which suggested to her that he was furious. Furthermore, she didn't feel she could blame him, since he had always been meticulous about contacting her well in advance in similar situations. Also, telling him that she had simply forgotten about him and the opera date because of a medical emergency was scarcely likely to prove a comfort to a male accustomed to the very best treatment when it came to the female sex.

By the time the taxi trundled up the long driveway to the imposing villa, Ella was very tense, because she was running against the clock and not doing very well. She rang the bell and, after a few moments, the housekeeper appeared, and her look of consternation was sufficient to warn Ella that her arrival was unexpected. Ella hastened past the older woman with a muttered explanation and apology. She sped upstairs, where she assumed her evening gown awaited her. There was no sign of it in the master bedroom, but she stilled in surprise on the threshold when she saw the scattered pieces of female clothing littering the floor. She frowned at the sight of the frilly black-and-turquoise bra and matching knickers, and wondered who on earth they could belong to. Unfortunately, she did not have to wonder for long.

The mystery was immediately solved when the bathroom door opened and a breathtakingly lovely blonde appeared, wearing only a towel. It was difficult to say which of them was the most discomposed by the unexpected meeting.

'Who are you? What are you doing in here?' Ella heard herself demand.

Aqua-green eyes challenged her. 'As I was here first, I could ask you the same thing.'

And, even as Ella parted her lips to speak again, a sick sensation took up residence in her tummy and perspiration beaded her brow. She wondered if she was the only woman in the world stupid enough to ask a beautiful half-naked woman what she was doing in her lover's bedroom. After all, the answer was so obvious the question didn't need asking. Striving to save a little dignity in a confrontation that had burst upon her with the abruptness of an earthquake, Ella retreated back to the doorway. She discovered that it was horrendously difficult for her to peel her stunned eyes from the blonde in the towel. A revolting, terrifying curiosity had her staring, and striving not to make bland comparisons. Her mind marched on regardless: she herself was older, less exciting in the curves department and, although her skin was good, she knew it wasn't quite as flawless. Rejecting those crazy, unsavoury evaluations, she spun on her heel and headed down the sweeping stairs at such a speed that she almost tripped over her own feet.

'Dr Smithson.' The housekeeper began speaking anxiously to Ella as she threw open the front door for herself, simply eager to be gone and leave the scene of her humiliation behind her. 'I'm sorry, but I didn't know you were coming.'

'It's okay. I'm fine,' Ella burbled, not wishing to deal with the woman's visible embarrassment. It was obvious that the housekeeper had a very good idea of what Ella had found upstairs. She just fled, hurrying down the drive as though a gale-force wind was powering her from behind. Her mind was a total blank. She didn't know what she was doing. She didn't know where she was going either. Shock had wiped her thoughts out, and fear of the pain of those thoughts was protecting her from them.

Aristandros had another woman. *Well, whoopee, Ella—what were you expecting? Did you think he had signed a one-woman-only pledge just because he had taken up with you?* It was not as if Aristandros had promised to be faithful. Indeed, he had gone to some trouble to declare that he was promising her no such thing in that wretched agreement. For all she knew he had a stable of other women stashed around the globe at his various properties or, indeed available to come at a call whenever he felt like a little variety.

Aristandros had gone into his Athens headquarters today, finished his day's work during the afternoon and had then come home with or to the very beautiful blonde and gone to bed with her. The bed had been made again. So the very beautiful blonde was tidy as well as clean! She pictured Ari's housekeeper telling him what had happened and flinched. Seeing a bus trundling along the road in the distance, she speeded up to reach the stop and flagged it down. It didn't matter where it was going, just as long as it got her safely away from the vicinity of the villa where she might be seen. Her phone vibrated in her bag and she dug it out and, refusing to even look at the message, she switched it off. She wasn't in any fit state to deal with Aristandros.

It was a warm, humid evening. Ella felt hot and her skin felt clammy, though her teeth kept on threatening to chatter in shock. She got on the bus and sat down at the back, her body lurching and swaying as the vehicle swung round corners. Why was she so shocked when Aristandros had only done what had always come naturally to him? Such a very beautiful girl, as well. If a man had always wanted the diversity and excitement of other sexual partners, he was unlikely to change. And no doubt, if she asked him, he would be honest with her about it.

Her mind went into free fall at the thought of him being *that* honest with her. Any admission of infidelity would cut like a knife and leave scars, haunting her for ever. But the images already tormenting her were no more comforting, she acknowledged wretchedly, for the idea of Ari in another woman's arms was her worst nightmare and always had been. Now it had finally happened, she was reeling from the pain she was experiencing.

But wasn't the extent of that pain her own fault, a self-induced punishment? What woman in her right mind would have fallen in love with Aristandros Xenakis and hoped for a happy ending? Countless women had tried and failed with him. Yet she was still crazy about him. She had held nothing back. In fact, a week ago, when she had watched Ari building a sand-castle with Callie—a real boy-toy skyscraper version of a sandcastle—she had wondered if she had made an appalling mistake when she'd turned his marriage proposal down seven years back. She had wondered if, against the odds, they might have found happiness together. She had known that although she loved her career and lived for its challenges it had never brought her the sheer, soaring happiness, excitement and contentment that he could just with his presence.

Her cheeks were wet with tears when she climbed off the bus at the terminal. What was she planning to do— run away and leave Callie behind? That option was absolutely out of the question. Hadn't Ari already accused her of running away when anything upset her? Ella bristled at that recollection. But exactly what was she doing now? She couldn't give up on Callie; she just *couldn't*! Whatever happened, whatever else she had to bear, there was no way she could give up on the little girl she loved. At the same time, however, she needed a few hours' grace to pull herself back together before she had to face Aristandros again. She decided that the wisest option was to find a hotel for the night.

She walked for ages before she came on a small establishment sited in a quiet street. Checking in, she was conscious of the receptionist's swiftly veiled curiosity, and when she saw her reflection in the mirror in the *en suite* bathroom of her hotel room she grimaced in horrified embarrassment at the state of her face. Her mascara had run, and her eye shadow had smudged where she'd wiped her eyes, and her hair was all messy. She freshened up and then made herself switch her phone back on. She couldn't stage a vanishing act for very long. She had also left Aristandros standing at the opera. Although that was the very least of what he deserved, it would have gone down like a lead balloon.

Her phone rang within seconds of being switched on.

'Where the hell are you?' Aristandros growled.

'I'm sorry I didn't make it, but I need some space tonight.'

'No!' It was thunderous. 'No space allowed. Where are you?'

'In a hotel, a little place, not one you'd know. I really do need to be alone for a while,' Ella breathed flatly, wondering how she could possibly stand to be with him ever again, how she could ever contrive to live with him and the knowledge of his infidelity.

'You're not allowed to walk out on me under any circumstances,' Aristandros intoned in a fierce undertone. 'I will not tolerate it.'

'I'm not walking out on you.' Ella framed those words with a sob trapped in her throat.

'Ella…' he breathed huskily.

Ella cut the call before she could let her turbulent emotional mood betray her into revealing more than she should. But he would soon find out through his staff that she had met his trollop. No; where did she get off calling another woman a trollop just because she had slept with Ari? After all, she wasn't married to him. He was still a free agent in the eyes of the world.

Tears choking her, Ella, her slender body trembling, sank down on the end of the bed. As she always feared, her love for Aristandros was tearing her apart at the seams, destroying her strength and self-esteem, when really the only person she ought to be thinking about was Callie, who was safely asleep in her cot and blissfully ignorant of the messes adults could make of their relationships. But Ella recognised at that moment that she had to find a way to sort this mess out, because it was unlikely that she could trust Aristandros to make that effort.

More than an hour later, she jumped in surprise when a knock sounded at her door. Glancing out through the peephole, she could see nothing but a large probably male shape and she opened the door on the chain.

CHAPTER TEN

'OPEN the door, Ella,' Aristandros instructed harshly.

Ella was shattered that he had found her so quickly. She shut the door, undid the chain and opened the door again. 'How on earth did you know where I was?'

His tension palpable, Aristandros was staring at her, his brilliant dark gaze roving from the crown of her head down to her feet and swiftly back up again. 'I have tracking devices in your mobile phone and your watch, so it was just a matter of switching on the surveillance equipment to locate you—'

Ella gaped at him aghast. '*Tracking devices*?' she parrotted.

'A precaution in case you were kidnapped, a standard security procedure,' Aristandros proclaimed matter-of-factly. 'I'm a very wealthy man, and it's possible that someone could try to target you because of your connection to me.'

'You fixed tracking devices on me?' Ella condemned him in angry disbelief, still back at that first admission. 'And you never said a word about it either.'

'I didn't want to make you nervous or scared. But

I'm not going to apologise for it, either,' Aristandros added in an aggressive undertone. 'I needed to be sure you were as safe as I could make you. It's my job to protect you.'

'A tracking device,' Ella muttered shakily. 'Like I'm a possession…a stolen car or something.'

'You are a hell of a sight more important to me. It was no big deal until you went missing tonight and, let me tell you, you've put me through complete hell in the space of a few hours!'

Pale and drawn, Ella slowly breathed in. 'Have I really?'

'Why didn't you phone me from the hospital? You could have let me know what had happened, not cleared off in an air ambulance as if I didn't exist!' Aristandros launched at her, his strong bone-structure rigid beneath his bronzed skin. 'Ianthe was out and I couldn't get hold of her, so I had no idea an emergency had come up. All the domestic staff knew was that you had gone off somewhere with her. I was worried about you—'

'Why? What could possibly have happened to me on the island?' Ella couldn't believe she was managing to stay so calm.

Aristandros glowered at her as if that was a very stupid question. 'You could have had an accident. I knew something must have gone badly wrong when you didn't show up at the opera house, because you're usually very reliable.'

'Oh…'

'And then Yannis phoned after you had left the hospital to rave about how wonderful you had been with his daughter, and I began to understand what had happened. But you never arrived at Drakon's house because he checked.'

'Drakon's house? Why would I have arrived there?' Ella questioned uncertainly.

'That's where you sent your dress.'

'Ianthe organised that.' Ella hesitated. 'I assumed it had been sent to the villa outside Athens.'

'Ianthe knew I had a bunch of guests staying there this week, so she wouldn't have sent it there.'

'Guests?' Ella echoed weakly.

'I understand that you may have met *one* of them,' Aristandros pointed out with laden emphasis.

Suddenly the atmosphere was so thick it could have been cut with a knife.

Ella was very still and she stood very straight. 'Is that what you call the young woman I met—a guest?'

'So you did rise—or should I say *sink*—to the worst possible conclusion,' Aristandros gathered, his sensual mouth compressed into a grim line of disapproval. 'Eda is my niece, the daughter of my father's youngest sister.'

Her stress level rising as his explanation gathered pace, Ella's brow had indented. 'Are you saying Eda was the girl I ran into? And that she's a relative of yours? If that's true, why was she in the master-bedroom *en suite*?'

'I have no idea. Her parents left her at the villa while they attended the opera because she refused to go. She's something of a handful, and fairly spoilt. Maybe she was trying out the facilities or just exploring while she had the house to herself. How should I know?'

Ella was mentally running through the explanation to see if it could fit what she had seen.

'You can ask her when you meet her tomorrow.'

'I'm going to meet her?' Ella framed uncertainly.

'I'm throwing a party on the island for my relatives tomorrow.'

As Ella began to hope that she had totally misinterpreted the girl's presence at the villa, her legs seemed to go hollow, and her head swam. That physical weakness was her body's response to the powerful rush of relief assailing her. 'Oh, my goodness,' she framed. 'I thought…'

Aristandros reached for her hands and pulled her closer. His dark-golden eyes were raw with reproach. 'Yes, you immediately assumed that I was *shagging* a sixteen-year-old behind your back!'

'She's only sixteen?' Ella mumbled, clinging to his hands to stay upright while she acknowledged that the girl had indeed looked very young.

'I prefer rather more mature specimens of womanhood, *khriso mou*,' Aristandros spelt out levelly. 'Although that does make me wonder why I'm with you, because sometimes you seem to react more like an impulsive airhead of a teenager than the intelligent adult I know you to be.'

A flood of hot moisture engulfed her eyes in a tide, and she blinked repeatedly while staring down at their still-linked hands. 'Her underwear was lying on the bedroom floor. She was only wearing a towel. I did think you must have been with her…'

'No.' His handsome jaw clenched. 'For that matter, I haven't been with anyone else since you came back into my life.'

Ella was so relieved by that admission that a sob escaped her. 'But that agreement said—'

'That was just me acting like a gorilla and beating my chest to ensure you had some healthy respect for me,' Aristandros admitted, gripping her hands so tightly in his that she was convinced they would go entirely numb. 'I'd like to go home now. I appreciate that it's late, but the helicopter is standing by at the airport, and I very much want to get back to the island tonight.'

'Okay.' Ella's voice was small and breathless, and she nodded in confirmation; the terrible, frightening tension and the fear of an unknown impossible future was leaving her piece by piece. There *was* no other woman in his life. He hadn't been with anyone but her since they'd got back together again. She had misunderstood, deemed him guilty when he was innocent. Her world had horizons and possibilities again, but she was almost afraid of accepting that fact.

'You're really shaken up,' Aristandros remarked, draping her bag over her shoulder and guiding her out of the room. 'I should be shouting at you for thinking the worst of me and putting me through a hellish evening of frustration and worry. I don't even like opera at the best of times, but tonight I felt trapped.'

'I'm sorry,' she muttered in the lift, and she wanted to lean up against him and cling but wouldn't let herself act that weak and feminine.

'You're never going to trust me, are you? Why do I get the feeling that I'm paying for your stepfather's sins?'

Ella ducked her head as he tucked her into the limo waiting outside. She had made a hash of things again. A sniff escaped her and then another. Aristandros wrapped both arms round her and almost squeezed the life's breath out of her. 'Don't be silly. You have nothing to cry about.'

'Maybe it was stupid, and I know I misunderstood, but I honestly thought you must have slept with her I was devastated!' Ella gasped out strickenly. 'And I didn't know what I was going to do because I couldn't give up Callie to walk away from you—I *couldn't*!'

Aristandros held her back from him. 'That's one worry you don't have to have ever again.'

'What do you mean?'

'I care too much about Callie to use her to control you. You were right. I shouldn't have involved her in our arrangement. That was inexcusable.' His darkly handsome features were taut and grim as he made that statement. 'Whatever happens between us, I will share custody of Callie with you. You love her and she loves you, and I have watched her blossom in your care. I will never try to separate you from her and you will both always enjoy my financial support.'

Ella was astonished by that far-reaching promise and the conviction with which he spoke. 'Why are you saying this now? Why have you changed your mind after forcing that iniquitous agreement on me?'

'I recognise that what I did was wrong from start to finish: using Callie as bait to trap you, forcing such an unscrupulous contract on you. Drakon was right in what he said, and he didn't know the half of what I imposed on you. Worst of all, I knew that what I was doing to you was wrong even as I did it. Yet I *still* went ahead with it,' Aristandros recounted heavily, his handsome head turned in profile to her, his mouth harshly compressed.

'Why, though? Was it all about revenge?' she pressed, desperate to understand what had motivated him

The silence lay like a blanket and the tension in his

big, powerful frame was so fierce she could feel it even though they were no longer touching. The limousine was already pulling in at the airport.

'Ari…?' she prompted. 'I need to know.'

'I told myself it was purely an act of revenge, but it wasn't. The truth is usually the most simple answer—and the simple answer is that I just wanted you, and that agreement bound you hand and foot to ensure you couldn't walk away again. I needed that protection before I could let myself get involved with you again,' he breathed in a driven undertone. 'But now I realise that I don't want to keep you only because I've got legal custody of your daughter.'

'So, if I want to leave and return to my life in London,' Ella whispered unevenly, 'You'll let me go and allow me to take Callie with me?'

'Letting you both go would kill me, but I won't go back on my word to you,' Aristandros declared with raw emphasis as the door beside her was whipped open by his driver.

Surrounded by his security team, they walked through the airport in silence. *I just wanted you.* Four little words that made a heck of a difference to Ella, and that kept on rhyming back and forth through her head, providing a much-needed mantra of hope. In spite of all the other options he must have had, he had returned to his past and blackmailed her back into a relationship with him. For the first time she registered that she had been and still evidently was much more important to Aristandros Xenakis than he had ever been willing to admit. He didn't want to lose either her or Callie, but he was willing to let them go free if that was what she decided she wanted.

As they waited in a VIP lounge, Ella was conscious of his scrutiny. She knew he was desperate to know what she intended to do next. He had removed the one threat that could have forced her to take whatever he threw at her. No longer did she need to stay with him purely for Callie's sake. His ferocious pride couldn't live with that concept. Blackmail, he had finally discovered, did have its drawbacks.

They were walking towards the helicopter with a neat, respectful space between them when Ella reached abruptly for a lean, brown hand across that divide. 'I want to stay with you,' she told him tautly.

Right there and then, Aristandros turned round and swept her straight into his arms, plunging his mouth down urgently on hers with a passion that blew her away. He had to practically carry her on board the helicopter after that. She was stunned by the level of his relief at her announcement, and could not have doubted his level of ongoing satisfaction over that news when he gave her a heart-stopping smile and retained a hold on her hand throughout the flight. The engine was so noisy that there was no chance of any further conversation until they arrived back on Lykos.

Ella kicked off her shoes just inside the front door when they arrived and padded off straight to the nursery to satisfy her desperate need to see Callie. When she looked up from the cot and the peacefully sleeping child, Aristandros was on the other side of it.

'I really screwed up tonight—the opera thing,' Ella said ruefully. 'I know it was important. I'm sorry I didn't make it.'

Aristandros gave her a wryly amused appraisal. 'You

left me standing. But then I'm used to you embarrassing me in front of my family.'

Ella blinked. 'Your…er…*family*?'

'Yes. Pretty much the whole tribe attended that benefit, and I was planning to show you off to them all.'

'My word; truthfully?' Ella prompted as she followed him out of the nursery. 'Why did you want to show me off?'

'Because I very much hope you're going to marry me, but I wasn't so stupid that I was going to make an announcement without thoroughly discussing terms with you in advance,' he explained smoothly.

Her bright-blue eyes grew very wide. 'You're proposing *again*?'

'A tactful woman would have left out that last word,' Aristandros told her, walking her out on to the terrace where a champagne bottle and glasses sat on the table. 'Are we celebrating or not?'

Ella winced. 'I'm totally, madly in love with you and just like the last time I really, really want to marry you and be with you for ever. But I also spent a large chunk of my life training to become a doctor.'

'And you can *still* be a doctor.' Aristandros frowned as she looked at him in shock. 'I was being very selfish, which I hate to admit comes naturally to me around you. My mother was so obsessed with the film world that she had no time or energy to spare even for me, never mind my father. I don't want a marriage like that. I once resented your medical career because you chose it over me.'

Her lovely face was pensive in the moonlight. 'No, I think I used it as my get-out clause because I'd suffered

Theo as a horrid example of a womaniser and I was so afraid of getting hurt. I should have had more faith in you.'

'We didn't have enough time together.' Aristandros lifted her hand and slid a ring on to her engagement finger. 'It's the same diamond I planned to give you seven years ago, but I've had it reset.'

'It's glorious.' Ella watched the glittering stone sparkle like starlight on her hand and a warm, deep sense of happiness began to fill her.

'We were too young then,' he admitted ruefully. 'If we'd been more mature we would have tried to find a compromise and a way of being together that we could both live with. Instead I lost my temper with you because you made me feel foolish, which was very superficial.'

'You really broke my heart,' Ella confided, ready to be totally frank now that she had his ring on her finger and a proper secure future to look forward to. 'I couldn't believe you'd ever loved me.'

'I loved you so much that I never found anyone else to replace you. With you I thought I could break the Xenakis tradition of bad marriages. I believed that settling down while I was still quite young into marriage would give me a much better prospect of happiness than, for instance, the life I've been leading since then.' His rich, golden eyes were full of regret. 'But I fell at the first challenge.'

Ella wrapped her arms round his neck, her fingers gently feathering through the silky, black hair at his nape. She wished she had understood him better seven years earlier and recognised that his troubled back-ground had made him crave a much more stable life with one woman rather than a succession. 'You were so all-or-nothing about everything, and then you just walked away from me and I never heard from you again.'

'You just walked away too,' he reminded her. 'I was too proud to chase after you, although I thought of looking you up when I was over in London at least fifty times.'

'There's never been anyone else for me. I never stopped loving you although I didn't realise that until recently.'

'I fell in love with you on our first date. You got drenched with sea spray and you laughed. Every other girl I knew would have thrown a fit.'

'I'm not vain, but I'm a jealous cat,' she warned him, cherishing the ease with which he could look back through those years and recall one tiny incident, in much the same way he had remembered her admiring comment about the church on Lykos. The idea that he loved her was becoming more and more real and credible with every passing second. She smiled, and soon discovered that she couldn't stop smiling.

'I've sown my wild oats, but I didn't enjoy myself so much that I want to do it again, *agapi mou*,' Aristandros confided with blunt sincerity. 'I wanted a second chance with you. I wanted to hear you say you'd misjudged me. But when I found out about your wife-beating stepfather I got a step closer to understanding why you were so unwilling to trust me. When you threw that jealous scene after the Ferrand party, I was overjoyed, because that proved that you still had feelings for me just as I did for you.'

'So, what do you want now?' Ella enquired tightly.

'All I really want now is more of what we already have. I'm very happy with you. To be frank, I was disappointed that you weren't pregnant. I want to have a baby with you.'

Ella released a happy sigh at the prospect and beamed at him. 'How soon can we start trying?'

Aristandros laughed with rich appreciation. 'Would tonight be too soon?'

Ella regarded him with eyes as starry as the night sky above. 'No; I'm available without appointment whenever you want.'

'I should warn you that I want you pretty much all the time, *latria mou*,' Aristandros admitted, bending down to press his mouth to hers and kissing her slowly and skilfully until the blood drummed through her veins in a passionate response. 'It's an effort to go away on business when I've got you in my bed.'

'I don't want you going anywhere right now,' Ella confessed, her hands curling into the lapels of his suit jacket at the mere mention of him needing to go away from her. 'I want you all to myself. Will we get married on the island?'

'Yes. And soon,' he urged. 'Speaking as a guy who was once engaged for about five minutes, I don't believe in long engagements.'

'Neither do I,' Ella agreed fervently, while she busily thought about wedding dresses and Callie as a little flower girl, not to mention the provision of a baby to keep Callie company. She was so happy at the prospect of those delights that her heart felt as though it was overflowing.

Fourteen months later, Ella watched Kasma tuck Ari's son and heir, Nikolos, into his cot.

At three months old, Nikolos was already revealing Xenakis traits of character. He was very impatient, and screamed the place down if he wasn't fed immediately if he felt hungry. He truly adored an audience of female admirers and basked in their attention. He was advanced for his age in size and development. He already looked as though he was likely to be as tall as his father, and he had definitely inherited his father's heartbreakingly charismatic smile.

These days Drakon Xenakis spent more time on Lykos than in Athens. He was enchanted by his grandson's perfectly ordinary family life with Ella, Callie and the new baby. It was what he himself had never managed to achieve with his own late wife and children, and he appreciated the commitment it took for such a busy couple to make it work.

The house had been virtually rebuilt during the extensive renovations Ella had organised and was now a much more comfortable family-orientated home. It had not been easy to live in the house while all the work had still been going on, particularly while Ella was pregnant, but with her mother's help, and that of the staff, Ella had managed.

Jane had got divorced. Theo was still in prison serving time for that final assault on his ex-wife, while Jane lived in a city apartment and enjoyed a healthy circle of friends with whom she shared interests. At least once a month the older woman visited her daughter and, if both Ella and Aristandros were abroad together, she came to stay and took charge of the household.

But actually Aristandros was travelling a great deal less than he once had and worked more from home, while Ella was putting in part-time hours as the island doctor and taking an interest in the charitable endeavours of the Xenakis Foundation. Just as Aristandros had gone to a good deal of trouble to ensure that business rarely parted them, Ella had been equally careful to ensure that her job didn't steal too big a slice of her time and energy, and after a year she reckoned that she had got the balance exactly right. Plentiful help on the home front had been invaluable, and Callie currently attended a play group in town several mornings a week. That winter the whole family would be moving to the Athens villa to enable Ella to undertake a paediatrics course at the hospital.

Ella was blissfully happy. She and Aristandros had enjoyed a huge engagement party, and her wedding a couple of months afterwards had been the fairy-tale event that she had always secretly dreamt of having. Although Ella had been just a little pregnant at the time, she hadn't been showing. Lily had been her chief bridesmaid, and was currently applying for a surgical job at a Greek hospital after meeting up with a Greek businessman of her own at the wedding.

Ella had been surprised when she'd fallen pregnant so quickly, while Ari had merely had his unshakeable faith in his own virility proven to his full satisfaction. Callie was just at the age when a baby brother was a source of fascination to her, and had had to be dissuaded from treating Nikolos like a living, breathing doll. Ella and Aristandros had formally adopted Callie, and although they were careful to tell the child only as much as she could currently understand about her true beginnings and Timon, the little girl regarded them as her mother and father.

When Ella heard the buzz of the helicopter passing overhead, she grinned and headed out to the terrace to watch it land. Lean, dark and stunningly handsome in his business suit, Aristandros strode towards her.

'How was New York?' she asked.

'I had a frantic schedule. I'm just glad to be home with my beautiful wife and children.' As Callie raced towards him chattering in excitement, Aristandros swung the little girl up and hugged her with an ease that would have been foreign to him a year earlier. He paused beside Ella and lowered his dark head to kiss her.

Tingles of sensual awareness ran up and down her spine and into more private places. 'I like the dress,' he growled.

'Daddy's talking like a bear,' Callie giggled, sliding down to the ground to run off again.

Ella twirled so that Aristandros got the full effect of the short, red strappy dress swirling round her slim legs. 'Happy anniversary,' she told him.

'What's on the agenda for tonight?'

'Dinner on the yacht, and we're spending the night on board so that we can have lots and lots of private time without being interrupted,' Ella told him cheerfully.

Her candour brought a deeply amused smile to his striking features. 'You know how to keep me happy.'

'I certainly hope so. I love you loads,' she confided, wrapping her arms round him.

'And I love the way you love me as much as I love you.' Aristandros gazed down at her with brilliant dark eyes. 'I want you to know that this has been the happiest year of my entire life, *agapi mou*.'

Ella knew that that was an admission to be truly treasured, and felt almost overwhelmed by emotion.

Over dinner on *Hellenic Lady*, they caught up after his three-day absence and he gave her a sapphire eternity-ring engraved with their son's name. Hand-in-hand they walked to their state room, which was adorned with fresh flowers, to share a wonderful night together, and an early morning disturbed neither by a baby's cries for attention nor a toddler's wistful demands for company.

But that rare silence felt a touch weird to both of them and, after a quick breakfast, they got in the speedboat to sail back to shore and they spent the rest of the day on the beach as a family…

Rich, successful and gorgeous…

These Australian men clearly need wives!

Featuring:

THE WEALTHY AUSTRALIAN'S PROPOSAL
by Margaret Way

THE BILLIONAIRE CLAIMS HIS WIFE
by Amy Andrews

INHERITED BY THE BILLIONAIRE
by Jennie Adams

Available 21st August 2009

www.millsandboon.co.uk